# THE NEFERTITI LOOK

For Bill Latta
The Thistledown Reading
April 8, 1988

Cecelia Frey

Donated to
Augustana University College
by

William C. Latta

# THE NEFERTITI LOOK

## CECELIA FREY

**THISTLEDOWN PRESS**

Canadian Cataloguing in Publication Data

Frey, Cecelia
  The Nefertiti look
  1st ed. --

ISBN 0-920633-40-4 (bound).
ISBN 0-920633-41-2 (pbk.)

I. Title.
PS8561.R456N4 1987 C813'.54 C87-098104-8
PR9199.3.F73N4 1987


Book design by A.M. Forrie
Cover painting by Iris Hauser

Typesetting by Apex Graphics, Saskatoon

Printed and Bound in Canada by
Hignell Printing Limited, Winnipeg

Thistledown Press Ltd.
668 East Place
Saskatoon, Saskatchewan
S7J 2Z5


Acknowledgements

Some of these stories have appeared in the following periodicals: *The Dalhousie Review, Dandelion, Wascana Review, Whetstone, The Dinosaur Review, The New Quarterly,* and on CBC's "Anthology".

The author wishes to acknowledge the assistance of Alberta Culture in writing this book.

This book has been published with the assistance of the Canada Council and the Saskatchewan Arts Board.

**for fathers and sons**

*...The past is immortalized; that is to say, it is dead; and death is the root of all godliness and all abiding significance. . . . Yet Cornelius, pondering there in the dark, descries something not perfectly right and good in his love. Theoretically, in the interests of science, he admits it to himself. There is something ulterior about it, in the nature of it; that something is hostility, hostility against the history of today, which is still in the making and thus not history at all, in behalf of the genuine history that has already happened — that is to say, death.*

Thomas Mann, "Disorder and Early Sorrow"

*People aren't supposed to look back. I'm certainly not going to do it anymore. I've finished my war book now. The next one I write is going to be fun.*
Kurt Vonnegut, Jr., *Slaughterhouse Five*

# CONTENTS

## The Father

Kate went into her father's room. It was dark there, and cold. She stood by the bed and peeled back her overshirt, flannel, for the damp. She dropped it to the floor. In a slow stretching movement, she lifted her arms and pulled her undershirt over her head. She dropped this, too, to the floor. She unwound the layers of her skirt – she had sewn it to wrap around her two and a half times. She stood naked a moment, her white skin raised to the cold. As she slipped between the clammy sheets, her skin shuddered.

She folded her hands and waited. Soon his familiar bent shape would appear at the edge of the narrow bed. He would stand there saying nothing, doing nothing, but she knew what he wanted. She felt heavy with sadness. Still, it did not occur to her to refuse. She loved him too much.

She could hear the rain on the roof, on the windows, of her small brown house. She closed her eyes and saw herself creeping out the door, along the shadows of the road to the village and beyond. She watched the rain beat into the earth over his grave. It seemed to be beating down on her.

Tonight he was taking a long time. Sometimes he did, as though he had to come from a further distance. But she knew all she had to do was be patient. He always came after the drowning. Last night she had dreamed it again, more vividly than if she had been there. Sky and water boiled together, dark as ink. Wind, rain, lashed the boat, lashed her father's head lifted and dropped by the waves. Her uncle fought the waves but he was so small, the boat, the oars so helpless. Kate felt the panic of her father's body caught as it was with the sea twisting around it. She felt the terror of his hands, closing on nothing but water.

No one saw the drowning, but the story ran like a dose of salts, as Millie Spencer put it, through the village. The two men were out in a boat. The father went for a swim and got a cramp. The uncle saved him.

"What gets me," said Millie to her husband as she dished out his cod and poached egg that evening, "is why anyone in his condition would be out swimming in the first place."

"The poor bastard," answered her husband, gazing down at the egg, bald and bulging as the eye of a squid. "Maybe he was saved by mistake."

"Shhh," said Millie. "Don't talk that way."

People in the village never saw the father. Some doubted his existence. But Millie said he was the reason they had come here, for his health, and a beachcomber, coming in with some logs, made a positive identification. "Right on the sea ledge," he said. "Through the mist. I'm pretty sure it was a man." He raised his arm for another round. "Or else the goddamnedest biggest seabird I ever saw."

This sighting must have been before the father got worse. Towards the end, all he did was lie on his bed in his room. Millie told them this. She knew because sometimes she walked out to visit the mother. However, Millie did confess under direct questioning that she never actually saw the father. She did say she heard him once, laughing to himself.

"Kind of weird, like," she said. "Not a real laugh, because the paralysis got his throat. I could tell it bothered her something awful, so I pretended not to hear."


As soon as the father was dead and properly buried, Kate's mother set her sights on Vancouver. She had once been a nurse. Iris spoke of refresher courses and jobs. "The city," she tried to explain to Kate, "you know, you can go to the movies, and shopping. They have those big stores. And there's Stanley Park. I think it would be better for us, healthier you know, if we...I just thought..."

Those were the days when Kate, her face a complete blank, would stare in silence at Iris, daring her to speak and make a fool of herself. Later, Iris was able to ignore Kate's demands for her perfection. "The only way to satisfy you is to die!" she once shouted, at her wit's end.

The cows and chickens had been sold, the uncle and a grandmother returned to the prairies, to where there was a real farm and real people, the people in the pictures. After Iris went to Vancouver, they sent Kate letters from time to time and stuck ten and twenty dollar bills inside the folded paper. The money she put in a box on her kitchen shelf beside the tarragon and basil. In summer, these herbs gone wild steeped in the moist air surrounding the house, their scent an invisible membrane. In fall, Kate clipped them and hung them in her window to dry. In winter, she placed them carefully in clean jars.

The letters she was careful to answer. She was afraid if she didn't, they would come and haul her away. They asked how the sale of the acreage was coming along and wondered when she was coming home. She told them there'd been a lot of rain and fog. She told them she had just returned from walking to the village for groceries and the mail, that she was happy to receive their letters. She did not tell them that on the way home she had seen her father, plain as plain, standing on the cliff, leaning on his cane, looking out to sea, that he had turned and held out his hand. It had been as cold as when he was alive.

She wrote how much she enjoyed her pictures, taken during the good years when they had all been happy together. She did not tell them that she spent hours every day sorting them.

One shoebox contained her mother and food. Her mother was beautiful, pale and calm. Her hair was long, twisted into a roll on her neck. She wore loose dresses, more like robes. She moved all in one piece, bearing endless heaped platters to the table, presenting a series of birthday cakes with increasing numbers of candles.

A section of another box was devoted to a horse, the beautiful white horse of Kate's childhood. Often, through some uncanny trick of the camera, two horses appeared, or a horse and a person on top of each other, or a white unfocused blotch. Still, Kate never threw any of her pictures out. They returned her to a time when she rode with the wind in her hair across clear pastures.

She had five rolls of cousin Nan's wedding. Everyone was smiling; everyone was combed and buttoned; everyone was dressed so nicely. Nan was so beautiful in her gown. Once, after the father died and the housecleaning began, Iris was going through what she called a pile of junk. She looked at these pictures and said, "Oh, cripey, there's Nan's wedding. Lucky she wasn't showing yet. And your uncle Joe, he never could hold his booze. Some wedding dance, him shouting how he'd go outside with anybody." Of the pictures of her young self, she said, "Ugh. Fat," and, "Honestly Kate, you have to learn how to hold a camera straight. People will think I was forever at the kitchen brandy." When she got to the horse and called it a sway-backed, knobble-kneed monstrosity with worms, Kate gathered the pictures up and never let anybody look at them again.

Iris didn't know why Kate had to be the way she was. "The trouble with you," she shouted, "you're always floating around in some dream."

That was when they used to have terrible fights. They raged around the house, screaming their pain of loss. They threw things. A wooden spoon chipped the wallboard by the side of Kate's head. An iron dented the linoleum at Iris's feet.

"You killed him!" Kate accused.

"He died in his sleep!"

"You gave him the pills!"

"The doctor prescribed them!"

"You were jealous!"

"You're imagining things!"

"He wanted to live. You drugged him!"

Iris tried reason. "It's all history now, Kate. We have to go on. I did the best I could."

They both fell back exhausted.

Then suddenly Kate stopped fighting.

"I don't know what's got into her," Iris confided to Millie. "She's got real quiet. It's scary."

"When exactly did it happen?" asked Millie.

After Kate saw Iris off on the ferry, she walked home, went into her house and shut the door. She went through the kitchen, through a central hall, and into her father's room. She looked around her and felt strong. Once she had been weak, right after he died. They had descended upon his room with mops and pails and disinfectant. She was not able to stop them. In fact, she was the one who washed everything, dipping the rag again and again into the hot soapy water, throwing the water down the toilet. She had to. Otherwise, they would have done it and in the end caused more damage. She, at least, was able to save a few remnants, a half-used notepad, paper clips, rubber bands, a broken comb. She placed these things in a cardboard box and hid it upstairs under her bed.

She remembered when she had just finished the cleaning. She was standing much as she was now, looking at the bare mattress, the bare chair and night table. It seemed for a moment as though all traces of her father had been removed. Then she felt his presence fill the room, like God in church. At that sacred moment, Iris burst in, a whirlwind of energy and destruction. She flung open the window.

"We have to get rid of this closeness," she said, wrinkling her face. She turned and looked at Kate. "Oh, I know it's difficult, dear." She pulled Kate's stiff body down onto the mattress and tried to hold her. "But don't you think we talked about this? He expected me to carry on, to manage things... After all, I knew your father better than you did."

Kate would never forgive Iris for that. But now she could be generous. She had won. She had him all to herself. She thought how, coming home from school, she used to look forward to this room and him, so much that sometimes she had felt weak, almost sick. She had hated school because it kept her away from him. She had liked reading because they did that together, in this room. Her favourites were dark tales full of castles and ladies in towers. Her father had been an English teacher; he liked Shakespeare. She tried to like him too. But mostly, she couldn't understand a word of it, except for Ophelia with her flowers.

As Kate stared into the shadows, she saw a darker shape. It was her father. She could never mistake his straight black hair, his deep brown eyes, his lips, the way they sloped at the edges. His head was bowed, his face sad.

At first she was surprised but then she knew. "You couldn't come when she was here," she whispered. "I understand."

He stood silent and demanding. "It's all right," she said. "I know it was an accident. You didn't want to leave me."

Still, he did not go away. He seemed to want something more. "What is it?" she wondered. "What do you want me to do?" He opened his mouth. Out of it came a hollow whistle.

The spring evening a knock came at the door, Kate had her pictures spread on the kitchen table like a game of solitaire. At first, she was not going to answer, but then the knock came a second and third time.

She could not see Gerry. The light was behind him. She knew it was a man, that he was tall and thin, that his voice was loud and insistently cheerful. She didn't know why he was here. Then he said Millie and she remembered.

"Oh, Millie..."

"Phoned, yeah, you know, she said about the grass and to brace some apple tree that cracked in the wind."

"But I didn't think... I told her..."

"She said you'd put me off. She said I should cut the grass anyway. That it's full of mosquitoes."

"Oh, well," Kate sighed. She showed him the toolshed, the scythe. "Just put it back," she said, "when you're finished." She meant, "Don't bother me," but an hour later he knocked again. She was standing by the stove, waiting for him to go away. By now it was almost dark.

"I'll come again tomorrow," he said. He looked past her, into the house, but she didn't think he would be able to see much.

Iris came up on the weekend. Through the window Kate saw Willie Frobisher's truck jerk to a stop and Iris get out lugging her suitcase. Kate was resigned to these invasions. This woman with wash-and-wear hair, short skirts and high heels, this woman who had a boyfriend and a Vancouver apartment, was not really her mother. All Kate demanded of this woman, mincing through the grass and wild weeds, was that she not come too often and that she always phone first.

"Whew!" said Iris, setting down her suitcase. Then, looking around, "It's like a morgue in this place." She walked through rooms, snapping up blinds. "How can you stand it so stuffy," she said, opening windows. "How can you stand it so cold," she said and turned up the heat. She squinted at Kate. "No wonder you have to wear all those layers of clothes."

On Sunday morning, against a background of country rock, Iris made coffee. Kate's manner of doing anything drove Iris frantic. "For heaven's sake, girl, move!" she would shout, grabbing the pot, the dishrag, the broom. Or, "Put some elbow grease into it." Or, "Take hold of it." She found it impossible to say what she really meant which was that Kate frightened her.

"Look," Iris said, sitting down at the table. "Why don't you just come for a visit. Only a visit." Kate looked at her hands. Iris sighed. "Sometimes," she said, "I think you want to be miserable."

Outside, the sun was shining, a round disc through a layer of gauze. Gerry was already at work, clipping the hedge. He had taken off his shirt. "Good build," said Iris. "And I like his looks in a man. Dark hair. What colour are his eyes?"

"I wouldn't know," said Kate. "Or care."

Iris glanced at Kate. "He needs someone to take care of him." She looked back out the window and her voice went soft. "Fatten him up a bit."

Kate pictured her mother's hands feeding her father—strong, capable hands moving serenely between a bowl and a mouth. That woman smelled of starch and incense. This one who smells of stale perfume, thought Kate, would feed anything that comes along.

"I suppose he's something you and Millie dreamed up," she said.

"I don't know a thing about him." Iris kept her face blank. "Except he's in pre-med and Millie got him a summer job at the drugstore. But if he's Millie's nephew, he must be okay."

"He talks too much. About himself. About other people."

"He's lonely. Is that a crime? He likes you. Is that also a crime?"

"He'd talk to anyone. He's a compulsive talker."

"For you that means he says more than two words at a time," said Iris. "In case you haven't heard, talking is normal. It's the way people communicate."

Kate got up and turned down the radio. She went and stood by the stove with her back to Iris. She pulled her sweater around her. There was a time when such a remark from Iris would have started a week-long fight, or a week-long silence after Kate stopped fighting in the open. There was a time when Iris, when people, were able to hurt her.

The morning of her father's death, Kate was upstairs in her room, a small attic room. She had just awakened. For a moment she was happy, warm and cozy in her own bed, the voices of her family coming up from the kitchen. Then she knew that something was wrong. He's dead, she thought. And then, no. She could not have slept through the night while he was dying downstairs. He wouldn't have died without telling her, without somehow letting her know. But something was different. He must be dead. She must go down. She must go down in her long white gown, down the steep stairs and across the cold linoleum. Her mother would be there, her eyes pale from crying. She would rise and drift toward Kate, draw her head down to her comforting smell. Her voice would be solemn. The grandmother would speak in her wise old way, "Ah well, there must be a reason for it all. God knows what's best." The uncle would raise his hands, palms down, over the empty cups and bowls. Then her mother would sit for a long time, pressing her hands into a white linen cloth over her face. The kettle would boil.

Kate's dream of death was punctured by voices. That was it! The voices rising through the floor vent were different. They were wrong. They were like the voices of people let out of prison.

When she arrived in the kitchen they were busy eating breakfast. "You have to eat," said her grandmother, a woman who had driven a taxi in Edmonton during the war, between husbands. "Keep up your strength."

Her uncle left almost immediately for town. He wanted to see about selling things.

"We have to clean the house," her mother said, jumping up from the table. "People will call." She tied a bright cloth around her hair and started taking down curtains.

Kate insisted later that no one told her that her father had died, but Iris always denied this.

"...we have to keep the place up," Iris was saying. "If we expect to sell it."

"I don't want him around," Kate said. "Spying on me."

"Oh for heaven's sake, girl! He's doing it for you! Don't you know anything about men?" Then, as though to herself, "Of course, how could you know."

"I wouldn't want to know," said Kate. "I'm not like you."

"They're not so bad," Iris thought out loud. "They only want to be held. In the end, that's what they all want. In the night, in the dark."

Iris invited Gerry in for coffee. Kate went into another room. Still, she could hear them, chattering away, their voices full of hope.

Some days Kate decided they might get through the summer. Gerry could have the outside and she would have the inside. Other days, it seemed too much. He slammed tools, lumber. He whistled. She would be sorting her pictures, but she had to watch him. He couldn't be trusted. He was gaining ground, little by little, pressing, pressing and pretending not to. He stood in the doorway, but he could stand there for hours talking. She could not shut the door because he was in it. She turned away and he followed. Only one step the first time, but she saw what would happen. For a while after that, she did not open the door.

She spoke to him through a window. He was painting a fence, painting it yellow when she wanted white.

"Yellow is brighter," he said.

"I like white," she said.

He slopped some white into the yellow and stirred it around with a stick. She didn't think it made much difference, but since the fence was a compromise she said nothing. He had wanted to paint the house, he and Iris. But Kate wouldn't hear of that.

He brought her some herbal tea and a special honey that they sold at the drugstore. It was supposed to be pure. He pushed these things through the window, into her hands. She put them on a back shelf.

He kept finding new things to do. The grass needed cutting again. The day was hot. He knocked at the door. She ran a glass of cold water from the tap. She handed it to him. He looked past her into the cool shadows. She pointed to the table. He was so grateful. He turned suddenly helpless, his voice persuasive. She found herself saying things. "My father gave me the camera," she said, gazing at the wall. "For my tenth birthday. But when he died, I stopped taking pictures."

"Why?" he asked, shifting his chair.

She looked at the window. "Things changed. People..." She gestured. "I don't know."

He leaned forward. His shoulders crossed the edge of the table. She drew back, alarmed. After he left, she felt that something dangerous had happened.

"You have to get rid of him," Kate said to Iris. "You can talk to Millie."

Iris was opening a tin of sardines. "You can't hurt people's feelings," she said.

"Nothing's sacred," said Kate, hesitating before the cutlery drawer. "To him, everything's a story."

Iris poured off the oil and dumped the sardines onto paper towels." What dark secrets do we have?" she said. She slipped two slices of bread into the toaster.

"He doesn't knock. One night last week he burst in."

She had been sorting her pictures. "What's that?" he had asked. "Hey, I like old pictures. Who are they?"

"He doesn't mean any harm," said Iris, gazing into the toaster. "He just gets carried away."

"He's always turning on lights. He acts as if he owns the place."

"How can you see in the dark?" he had asked. "Maybe you really are a witch." His voice had gone soft. He had stared. He had put out his hand. He had almost touched her.

"It has to stop," Kate said to Iris.

"He wants to take you away from here," said Iris. "What's wrong with that?"

"He's a fool," said Kate.

The toast popped. They sat down to supper.

Later, Gerry came out with a case of beer. He and Iris settled themselves at the kitchen table. Kate pretended to read. She could hear how Gerry manipulated the talk so it came around to the father.

"Pleurisy," Iris said. And after a pause, "It was hard, seeing him go like that. Not what finally got him, so much, but before..."

"I heard something." Gerry's voice was respectful.

"There's nothing wrong with it," said Iris. "Who wouldn't, with the strain?"

"That's what Millie said."

"And it wasn't...completely, or anything like that. He just went a little funny, like, at the end. The way he'd go on. So rambling and confused. And then his voice went, you know. You could scarcely make out a word."

"That's not true," said Kate from her corner. "How can you tell such lies. I understood him perfectly." She ran upstairs to her room.

"I forgot she was here," Iris said. "I've put my foot in it again. Like when I told her about the drowning. I know I shouldn't have. But in those days she could get me going something terrible. Well, miss smarty know-it-all, I said, and after I wondered how I could have done it. If he told you everything, I said, did he tell you he tried to drown himself?"

"How did she take it?" asked Gerry.

"That's when we stopped fighting," said Iris. "That's when she started scaring me. She's too much like her father. Her mind always on death."

"She shouldn't be here alone."

"What can I do? Bury myself here with her?"

"Here, she remembers too much."

"What can I do? You see how stubborn she is. I can't very well drag her kicking and screaming onto the ferry. She's an adult by law now."

"She has to get away from here."

"She won't leave. She can't believe he's dead. He didn't say good-bye."

After a moment, Iris continued. "It was the way he died. It's the not knowing that gets a person. He couldn't clear his lungs, see." And after another moment, "I always gave him a sleeping pill. Just one. The doctor ordered it. The bottle always sat on his night table.

"It hasn't been easy for me either, you know," Iris said. "That's what she doesn't realize. I've had to fight to get free."

Upstairs, Kate heard and thought how Iris was blabbing out their history to this stranger. How he was learning too much. But Gerry was like that. He caused people to reveal things.

Kate chose an evening. She took a white cloth and candles from the bottom drawer of her bureau. From the same drawer, she shook out a white robe. She combed down her hair and in it pinned a fresh spray of herbs. From beneath her bed, she took the box which was her defence against people and the world. She went down to the kitchen and picked up the phone. It took her a moment to remember how to dial.

She sat down at the table. Each thing had to be taken out of the box, held in her hand for a long time, turned over and over. Each thing had to be laid out on the kitchen table in a certain order. The last thing she removed, the first she put back, was always his comb. It still smelled of his hair, his skin. She held it to her lips and breathed in its smell. She closed her eyes and waited.

After awhile she heard the door; she felt the light. She felt Gerry's eyes staring, at her, at the table, at her pitiful scraps of nothing. For once he was speechless. She turned and let him see her face, her wild hair, her blank painted eyes.

All the next day, she imagined the talk in the village, rumours of her madness circulating with new energy. She didn't care. Maybe now, they would leave her alone. She thought of the stories he would tell to his university friends. "Let me tell you about this girl I met last summer," she heard him saying.

That evening, a damp chilly evening, Kate looked out her window and saw him. He was standing watching the house. He seemed to hesitate. He might have come closer and knocked at the door. But instead he turned away. He crossed the border of trees the other side of the road and disappeared into a ground mist. Before that though, it seemed to her that he moved his shoulders as though getting rid of something.

She turned into the shadows of her house and found her father there. He beckoned to her and she followed him into his room. She knew now what she had to do. It was as though her relationship with Gerry made everything clear. She took sheets, blankets, a chenille bedspread from a cupboard and made up the bed exactly as it used to be. She took off her clothes and lay down.

He was so frail, only skin and bones. She gathered his body into the circle of her arms. She was young and strong. She would give him her warmth, her life. In return, she felt his wisdom beyond life flow into her. They were truly one, part of each other, floating on what Kate vaguely thought of as a warm sea, rocking on waves of gentle motion.

But then she felt him change. His arms were around her and he was holding her too tightly. She looked at his face and saw only the outline of its bones. In the darkness, the place where his face should have been mirrored a pool of black light. She felt herself being pulled into this reflection. She could not move. She could not breathe. He was so strong, stronger than she.

She knew then that Iris was right. But it didn't matter. Knowing earlier that she would be caught like this, she would have made the same choice. And once made she could not turn back. There was no solution. She could see clearly now that her sorrow was just beginning.

## The Nefertiti Look

She seemed to be a very friendly person. The way she whispered and giggled on the stairs. Probably tipsy. Expecting a gentleman caller. The husband, conveniently out of the way, down at the old man's, across the hall, down for crib and beer. Collaborators in sin. Sin, an old-fashioned word. But oh the sleazy horror of it all! The depressing quality of their mean, shabby lives! He would leave this museum of horrors tomorrow. He would leave. And yet they seemed happy. The happy savages. Why were they happy while he was miserable? They didn't know any better. Did that make them innocent?

She reminded him of someone from his past, but he couldn't remember who. The minute he saw her, through the sea of bodies in the room, everything else blurred. Only her face was clear. That face, at the same time strong and fragile. How could it be?

Rita was her name. She called him a honey and made him get up and dance and made him eat all that kolbassa and cheese and said how he looked like he needed a proper meal. She said she liked men with big noses. She said all the corny things about big noses. She laughed at her own voice.

Orestes Kilpatrick was his name. His mother was a Classics professor at the University of Toronto and thought the name, Orestes, an enormous joke, defying the gods, as it were. His psychiatrist father, now dead, had never appreciated any sort of joke.

Ory lived on the ground floor at the back. To get there, he crossed the verandah, passed the murmuring doors of other tenants, passed the stairs rising up into darkness where Rita lived. Beyond the power of one dim bulb in fringed shade, where the hall faltered and came to a shadowy end, was Ory's door.

The small room smelled of tobacco, old paper, mould up from the cellar steps across the hall. The air was hazy with smoke and steam. Someone in the house was cooking macaroni. The mist oozed under his door.

His long loose frame was draped on a short couch, his feet extending over the arm. His skin was brown from working at the excavations. His brown hair was bleached from the sun of spring and early summer. His eyes were closed. He was concentrating on making things come out right.

"I'm reconstructing what I think is the garbage pit," he said at the party. They had asked him about his work. "No human bones, just animal bones," he said. For, like children, they wanted to know the gory details about skeletons and blood. He mentioned weapons, arrowheads. They liked that better than cups and utensils.

As usual there was someone who read a little. "They're always finding some new dinosaur bones, aren't they? It seems t'me I've read about that, up around Drumheller there, they're always finding some new dinosaur bones or something."

"Say Rita!" a blurred face called. "Here's a man's digging up old bones!"

"Hell, I got lotsa old bones. It's young bones I need."

Recalling, Ory massaged down the blood vessels either side his forehead.

And someone, someone else, a man's voice… "What kinda work is that anyways? Digging up old bones."

"Well if you ask me, it don't sound like any work for a man."

Maybe that wasn't anyone from this house, thought Ory. A lot of people were at that party, people from the whole town, the surrounding district. Parties are like that here. Everybody comes. Still, they're all the same. The people here are all the same. The consensus of opinion. A man's work is to farm. The earth is to plant and to sow, a practical commercial venture, in spite of their ironic comments about grain prices. Picking bones from the earth is to them like picking flowers. Men do not pick flowers.

How did I get caught in this place, he wondered. What have I got myself into? What has the university got me into? Where people don't know anything about art or history or the development of civilization. Not that he wasn't aware that such people existed. He had fully expected he might run into them in some remote village in Afghanistan or in the middle of the Kalahari. But in Canada, for Christ's sake! And not in some northern outpost. But a hundred miles from one of Canada's major cities! At least the books called it major.

All right. All right, he was not here to think about them. They did not matter. He was here to figure it out once and for all. To get things settled. To sort it all out, and re-sort and then re-sort again if necessary. Make it all come out right. Somehow. So he could end the pain in the miracle of thought and reason.

But the outrageous way she teased everyone! The old man. Calling him the old lover, telling him to put up or shut up. The scandalous things she said to anyone. "Hey you, there, you getting enough?" Then protesting that she meant the oysters. But all the time exposing... exposing... What was it someone told him about her? Her husband was on some sort of disability pension.

"Rita's always making cracks about how he's on the pension and she's on the pill," Ory heard a voice say. "She always has some smart answer like that for everyone on account of she's a beautician, that's swank for hairdresser, at Josie's, and that's how come she has that hair, she gets it done for free on account of the girls do each other's hair during slack times."

No. Stop. All right. The tennis court in the cool of the evening. At home. Yes. As good a place to start as any. White. Wholesome. Clean. Summer. But still cool enough to wear a sweater at first. The hollow thud of the ball bouncing. The plop of the racquet on the ball. Yes, it comes back. Red cindered walkways. Another couple on the next court. A sharp laugh. He remembered that, the sharp laugh. And voices carrying, confirming scores across the net.

His circular exercise was broken by distant doors closing and opening, guitar strings and stereos.

All Ory could hear of the music was the beat, the bass, the rhythmic thump. And the voices. Around him buzzed these pestilences. "...just remember to wake me up at seven-thirty but I don't hafta get up till eight so don't keep bugging me like you did this morning... jeez mom, it's not fair... rip off the bloody door why don'tcha... how are you anyways... oh surviving, surviving..."

He got up too quickly. He stood a moment hanging on to the air. He lurched to the sink. He turned the hot water tap. He watched the way the water came brown out of the tap and mixed with the brown stains of the sink and whirled away down into the brown pipe. He picked up a cup from the litter on the counter. He rummaged around and found a spoon. He threw some instant coffee into the cup. He held the cup under the tap. With one eye he peered into a cardboard milk carton. Almost gently, he set the furry sleeping creature back down on the counter.

It is extremely doubtful, he thought, that such remarks have anything to add to the reservoir of human knowledge. Yet, surviving. That's more than I can say. Survival of the fittest. Their progeny, not mine, will litter the earth. I shall become extinct.

A great wave of irony swept over him. Along with it came the need to cry. Instead, he lit a cigarette.

Where was I, he wondered. Had he got as far as the tennis courts in the early evening? Had he got to Eunice? No, not yet. All right then, Eunice. Time to tackle Eunice. A girl who spoke in a high clear voice. Whom he did not really know well after all, he decided, scowling down at a pile of dirty clothes on the floor to one side of the couch. If he had, could he have forced himself past... past what? He flung himself onto the couch. I don't know. Perhaps, the opaque, impenetrable crust of manner and speech. Did he read that somewhere? Or was it his? He didn't know anymore. He could no longer tell himself from his books.

What was it Rita said to him at that party? "Are you for real? Are you sure you're not just a bunch of words strung together?" She was joking, of course, but the others turned on him then. He could feel their suspicion, their animosity to something they did not understand. But Rita made another joke and the moment passed. After that, she was especially pleasant to him.

Still, a couple of times he found himself almost trembling with fright, not sure what she might do or say. She was the type of woman who would not wait. Eunice now, she waited for his advances, and he did advance too. But then... then what happened?

Ory held his face in his hands and squeezed his eyes tight. But he saw it anyway. His ridiculous situation. His retreat. His humiliation.

He was saved by a bump on the stairs. Voices. "...I lost my footing there, that's what I lost... didja hurt yourself?... no, I just lost my balance there... are you all right?..." And so, he thought, the husband safely away. The other will come soon now. He pulled his hands down on his face and made a sad mask.

A foot on the stairs. Soft but heavy. Ory saw a man's foot on the worn stair runner. He saw a man's hand, a broad, strong hand grasp the railing, worn from grasping hands. He saw the riser wood gleam and a shoe, a work boot, black, unpolished. He heard a knock, a stealthy knock. Just before the announcer's voice on the radio next door turned suddenly loud.

Why is it so easy for them and so difficult for me? he called inside himself.

He lit another cigarette from the last. He stubbed the butt to death in the overflowing ashtray on the night stand.

Why don't I leave right now, tomorrow, he wondered. I need a city to get lost in. Here, moment by moment I am receding, evaporating into air like those glaciers I like to read about. Soon there will be nothing left. I must leave. I must finish this reconstruction as soon as possible and leave. In the meantime, I must leave this house. There must be other places in this town. There must be other rooms. That's settled then.

He felt better. He took in a deep full breath. In the middle of it, he stopped and exhaled quickly, suddenly fatigued. He was tired. Tired of it all. Need. Desire. He spelled it out to himself. I do not want to need or desire. I do not want to be needed or desired. Desire can be dangerous, desire can become twisted.

Overhead, he heard a footstep and a whisper. He sprang up, lifted his jacket from the hook by the bed, slammed the door as he left. With long-legged gait he walked the streets of the town. He tried The Blue Moon. The waitress had to interrupt her conversation with a man to bring Ory a cup of coffee. She went back to her friend and the two looked at him and laughed. Other people came in. They all laughed and talked in loud voices. "...d'y'want some? Help yourself... I already did, wanta ask another foolish question." They all found this exchange extremely funny.

Ory felt their eyes solid as a wall. He was a stranger. No matter that he was harmless, that in spite of his apparent youth he was a fossilized relic.

As he walked back to the rooming house, it started to rain. There was a time, he thought, when I had friends. I could get as drunk as anybody then.

Rita was waiting for him. On the verandah, looking out at the rain. She said hello and stopped him with her hand. He could not control the tic at the side of his mouth.

"Smell the rain," she commanded. Obediently, he lifted his head. "When I was a young girl," she said, and since she was not looking at him he could bear to look at her. From the front room a light shone out into the darkness onto her face. That face, where had he seen it before? That face, at the same time bold and shy. She wanted to talk. It would be rude to leave her.

"In the warm summer rain," she said. "I would take off my clothes. I don't do that now."

Why don't I touch her, he thought. What keeps me from it? What's wrong with me?

That night was the beginning of his dream. He was undressing Rita. In slow motion. By morning when he woke up he was still not finished. He closed his eyes and pulled the blanket over his head. But it was no good. He could not get his dream back. He tried to merely think the dream. But that was no good either. It was not real.

When he was fully awake, in the cold clear light of the day, he was ashamed of his dream. He vowed never to do it again, never to so much as touch Rita with his little finger. But he could not stop the dreams. He tried to discipline his mind before sleep. He dictated to his subconscious the substance of what his dreams should be. Still, he saw that face. He saw the vibrant colours. The warm living stone. She was lying on his bed. She was naked. The sheets were purple satin.

He tore her apart. That atrocious hair. That made-up face. Those eyebrows. Those lips. Who knew what was under all that paint and affectation. Probably some old hag. She was old. She could easily be in her late thirties.

Ory's rage exploded inside him and sifted down as gauzy fantasies. That she could be alive, that she could suffer, that life could have its way with her, while she remained proud and enduring.

He reined himself up short and turned in the other direction. Her dress, her grammar, her brashness; she lay in ruins at his feet.

Still, there was her excruciatingly painful fragility.

The day rained and rained, a constant, gruel-like drizzle. The digs had to be shut down. He sat all day in the shed that was his workroom. He sat bent over his work table, sorting and classifying life from another age. They don't know how lucky they are, he thought, safely and comfortably dead.

In the evenings he put off going to bed. Perhaps if he was tired enough he would not dream, or would not remember. He read until his eyes ached and his vision blurred. Maybe I'm going blind, he thought. But how can I keep on with my work if I'm blind? He saw himself standing before a huge mound of earth. Someone approached with a piece of bone. The renowned expert examined it with his super-sensitive fingers. It's a miracle, they all murmured, how he can... Oh Christ. Oh Christ, Kilpatrick. You're NUTS!

He must, he simply MUST get his nerves together. His work was suffering. He found it difficult to make decisions. He wondered if he was too conscientious. But, he argued with himself, what if I pass over something that is important? On the other hand, what if I give something importance that really has no importance? Or, worst of all, what if none of it is important?

Another evening he bought a large bottle of whiskey and drank it while staring dully at the bare brindle walls. He turned on his small radio. Through an alcoholic haze things became exceedingly clear. He decided to make a list, while everything was so clear. Observation and Evaluation of Primal Interaction in the Lower Socio-Economic Sub-Culture. But how can I make a list without including Rita? Into his momentarily unguarded mind came a clear vision of Rita's legs flashing up the stairs, opening, closing, opening.

He took a drink from the bottle. Clutching the bottle he got up and went over to the sink. He looked at his face in the mirror. He saw Rita's face, her face inside her face, one face after another, the faces growing smaller, travelling backwards.

Hard pounding feet on the stairs. Great shrieks and shouts from above stairs. At least the newlyweds at the front were quiet. Across the hall, the old man and his cronies, a constant low rumble of voices erupting occasionally with speculations as to whether that time they drank eleven cases of beer and caught four trout or drank four cases and caught eleven trout.

"Hey," screeched someone. "Get the lead out, willya! I can't stand here with my legs crossed all night!" Someone sang "Ave Maria". The voice could not quite make the high notes.

Ory's radio sputtered and died. Finally, the house became quiet. It darkened. It slept. Ory passed out while scowling at a fly buzzing at his window. Dreams ravaged his mind. More clearly than ever.

He avoided the house. For days at a time, he spoke to no one. He forgot to eat. He became a shadow that no one saw. He worked with greater and greater intensity, late into the dusk of the long northern evenings. He wheeled his bicycle out from behind the shed, swung his leg over the saddle, and bumped along the country ruts. The lights of the town were ahead. Saturday night and some sort of carnival or stampede. He recalled colourful posters plastered up on storefronts and fences. The streets were busy with traffic and people carrying teddy bears and flags and wearing straw hats. Why can't I join them? What is wrong with me that I cannot enjoy myself like any normal human being? See these men. Just ordinary men. Half cut. Having fun. What's wrong with me?

He passed a park and the streets became quiet. He rattled past a darkened store window, past a silent cavernous alley. He noticed nothing. He was thinking about becoming the greatest archaeologist who ever lived, devoting his entire loveless self to his work. Why not? A monk of sorts. He saw himself lecturing at the great universities of the world, holding up his hands to standing ovations. At least in the city, at the university, there was an intellectual communication. Occasionally, yes, he would say, in discussing something of mutual interest, there was a close feeling of intellectual understanding between two people.

He wheeled his bicycle up through the old man's garden. He crossed the yellow slab of light from the old man's window. From the house came sounds of voices and music. Through the window, he could see people, sitting, standing, dancing. Of course, carnival. They never needed much excuse for a party. He went in the back door, hoping no one would notice. But no, here came the old man, out of his place, through his open doorway.

"Come in, come on in," he gestured. "Jesus, whatcha doin'? Come on in."

The old man would not hear of an excuse. He came down the hall, put his bearish arm around Ory's shoulders. "Jesus," he said in his low throaty growl. "A man needs something, y'know, a little something to keep him warm, like."

From the doorway Ory saw a rush of colour, a flurry of activity. He heard a jangle of sound. Loud music on the stereo confused his judgement. A woman in a sheer red harem costume danced. A strongman flexed his muscles. Someone, grotesque and cackling, leaned forward. As for the old man, that old scoundrel wore his brown gardening hat and waved a stick. "Come on, come on in there, you. Ladies and gentlemen, I believe you have all met our new roomer. Step right in there, don't let us scare you away, oh no, we're not so bad."

"Clodhoppers," chuckled someone softly. "Just a buncha clodhoppers. Nothin t'be scared of."

"Get him some rum," ordered the old man. "Or we have gin, plenty gin, we got everything tonight. Oh yeah, give it to him straight, oh that's good, that's good stuff. That'll put hair on your chest, that'll warm up the inside, now we gotta find you a nice girl for the outside, eh, oh you're gonna be thanking me in the morning."

Someone flashed a deck of cards. Someone looked up from the ouija board.

Ory knew that if he did not leave this instant something terrible would happen. He turned, but Rita grabbed his hand and pulled him to the couch, down beside her. She moved her leg against his. His leg jerked in a spasm before scuttling sideways. She laughed. The room turned. Lights? Or Rita's legs?

He closed his eyes to steady himself. Starting pinpoints of light, red at the centre, grew large, golden, burst darkly. What had they given him? What had they put in his drink? Someone replaced the empty glass in his hand with a full one. His only thought was to return, safe and sound, to his room. He drank down his whiskey too quickly. Everything was a whirl of glitter. If only the whiskey would stop. If only Rita would stop. Instead, she pressed closer. He felt ill.

Someone wanted him to pick a card, any card. People kept disappearing and reappearing. Where did they come from? Where did they go?

He studied the flight path, from this room, from his skin. Now it was clear to the door. If he could just get up and go out. Why not? No one would stop him. Why did he not get up and go back to his own room, or better still, continue out of this house and down the road and away forever?

He made his move. At the door, he looked back. No one seemed to have noticed. The ouija woman studied the board and planned her strategy. Some of the young people had gone to another party next door. The children were in the kitchen. The women gossiped.

Safe inside his room, except not safe. The room turned. Lights turned. Lights from the carnival. Across the river, through the trees, lights from the ferris wheel spun. Through his open window voices travelled. Through loudspeakers, voices of hucksters mixed with tinned music.

A knock came at his door. He knew who it was, and he was afraid, but still he answered. She came in. She moved toward the bed, switched on the bedlight, drew the curtain. The room was suddenly quiet and still. She turned slowly around. And he was caught again by that face that settled him into himself, that told him both his past and his future. But to find her here! In this house, this place, at the end of everything. Why could she not have been a young girl, pure and innocent, sitting in a field of daisies waiting for him, so that only his influence, his mark, would be upon her.

Rita closed in. She raised one arm, then the other. Ory knew that escape was impossible. But when he looked at her face, he saw that she forgave him everything. His dreams, Eunice, his Classics professor mother. In the light of such forgiveness what did it matter that he was a hostage in this place? What did it matter that the bones he dug up might prove to be worthless? What did it matter, when such forgiveness could always, each time, circle him back to the beginning?

## Tamar Ferouin Amongst the Savages

Horowitz pushed open his back gate and stepped into the alley. He was an old man who walked slowly and who, even on this balmy, cloudless June morning, wore a black coat and a peaked cap. Thrown across one shoulder was his bottle sack, burlap, looking somehow ridiculous the way it hung limp and empty. When he returned in a few hours it would be full, gorged with bottles and tins. This neighbourhood could be counted on for a good haul. The hand that held the sack was permanently stained by nicotine, earth, and general wear and tear. His smell was of old tobacco, old boiled meat and cabbage, and ultimately, simply plain old Horowitz.

In her still face, Esther Helge's eyes glinted steel. For one split-instant they opened and flickered, then they closed back over in appraisal. Watching Horowitz, through a breakfast nook window across the lane, Esther rested her arms on the table. A woman of medium height, broad but spare, her arms were covered down to her buttoned cuffs. She always wore stockings and laced oxfords, even around the house. Although her government pension was small, she allowed herself a permanent wave every six months and a blue rinse every six weeks. Every morning she dusted her face lightly with powder and spread her lips, one sweep in each direction, with sheer tint. She put one dab of cologne, spring bouquet, on each wrist. For, while she scorned women who tried to look younger than their years, she knew if she did not continue making an effort something terrible would happen, she was not sure what, some vague disaster that she sensed around her, ready to pounce, something that involved total confusion.

Horowitz's sack, advancing on its morning round of alleys and garbage tins, she saw as a retreat, both literally, as it disappeared down the lane, and also in the way it conveyed to her a sense of just how low a human creature could let himself get. Horowitz, the ragman, as he was known on these streets. He must have had other names at one time, but no one, not even Walter, knew what they were. His life, his other life, had happened so long ago that perhaps even he did not remember it.

Why he was known as the ragman when he collected bottles and tins, Esther did not know, nor did she care. What she did know was his smell, that it was brown and evil, and the look of his hands, his jagged black fingernails. Sometimes when she was out with Gertrude, the only way she would go out around here, they met him, and then they had to stop and talk.

One of the reasons you have to lock your doors in this neighborhood, Esther thought of Horowitz. Not that she was afraid of that old man, but the overly friendly were just as bad as the attackers. In fact, in their own way they did attack. But Gertrude didn't seem to mind being attacked. She'd talk to anyone, smile at anyone. Esther knew with certainty that some day her sister was going to regret doing this. It was true that Gertrude had been acting friendly for more than sixty years and nothing had happened yet, if you discounted Walter, who as far as Esther was concerned was disaster enough for any one woman.

Gertrude was in the kitchen, a cupboard area separated from the table by a counter. She had smaller bones than Esther, but she was fleshy, her flesh bouncing in the same rhythm as the plastic cylinders that covered her head and that had come loose in the night. Her grandchildren played around her knees, in her pathway. One cried and lifted his arms. Gertrude bent to pick him up, tossed him up onto the soft cushion of her shoulder. With the exertion, her face turned bright red. That woman, Esther decided, is going to drop dead from a stroke one of these days. Her own fault too, letting herself get like that. Low thyroid, Gertrude called it, but Esther knew that was just an excuse for being fat and for being so slow about making breakfast.

Not that Esther would have minded getting her own breakfast. And she was quite willing to help. But Gertrude always told her to sit down and rest her legs. Esther knew that Gertrude said that to get her out of the way, but she submitted to the lie. There wasn't room for both of them in the small U-shaped kitchen. Gertrude would be constantly running up against her the way she did with people, as though she did not know where her body ended and the other person's began. As children, she and Gertrude had shared the same bed, in winter cuddling together like puppies. Esther could no longer recall the feel of another human body, but she did not mind. The very thought of flesh touching flesh she found unnerving. When by accident she and Gertrude brushed arms or hands, she felt something like pain on her skin.

She did suppose, to be fair, that Gertrude's flesh did fill out skin and wrinkles. She looked down at her own arms. Beneath the cloth of her dress, her skin, she knew, hung down from the bone and spread in narrow folds on the table top. She moved her eyes to the distinct numbers on the face of her watch. Seven fifty-two. She wondered whether Walter would ever come to the end of yet another one of his anecdotes in which he played the leading man, and whether Gertrude would ever get that food on the table.

Not that she was hungry. She was never really hungry any more. And she never let herself get really full because that would mean discomfort. She only knew that one boiled egg and one piece of toast would get her through to lunch without feeling faint. There was a time when she was ravenous for meals. She would heap her plate, stuff herself, stretch her stomach. Then she would push back from the table feeling that she would never need to eat again, only to be starving five hours later. But that was when she chored for people, when she was young and on the farm, when she could feel her body, feel its needs and satisfactions.

Esther wanted to get breakfast over with so she could go up to her room, the only place in the house where she could expect even a minimum of peace and quiet, and accomplish something. Already that morning she had been inspired. It had come to her just like that, in between buttoning the front of her dress and arranging her hair and face before the mirror. She had jotted it down. "High cliffs towering to reach windy heights of undeniable truth." Now, watching Walter's mouth open and close like a trap, she wondered if "indisputable" would be better. She decided to change it as soon as she could. She was sure that this time she was really onto something. The way that line had come to her all of a piece, leaving her slightly awe-struck, seemed an omen. Not that she ever had much trouble with first lines.

"Beach, ceach, deach, leach," she thought. But it was no use. Walter's voice like radio static, Gertrude's slamming of cupboard doors, those

children... Why Gertrude thought it necessary to raise her grandchildren
after raising six of her own, Esther could never hope to imagine. In her
opinion, it was extremely irresponsible of Janine to keep having them,
especially since she had never bothered getting married. Esther suspected,
although when she brought the matter up Gertrude always looked away,
that there was more than one father involved, as well. But, Esther realized, Janine was like that. Nobody expected her to be responsible. There
was always somebody around for people like Janine, somebody else to
pick up the pieces. And you couldn't blame Janine, either. She only took
after her mother. Gertrude had been like that too. Soft, pretty Gertrude,
with large brown eyes and curly dark hair.

For a long time, when they were young, Esther wondered who Gertrude looked like. Then when their mother died and Esther was cleaning
out her things (no one else in the family felt up to it), she found some
old pictures, pictures of people left in the old country. From the name
on the back of one photograph, Esther recognized the aunt who in family
legends did such beautiful handwork. People like that, like that aunt, like
Gertrude, were allowed illusions of romance, allowed pretty clothes, parties, flirtations. People like that were not expected to hold down a job
for more than a few weeks at a time, were not expected to use what little
pay they earned on anybody but themselves. It had not seemed Gertrude's
fault that all the fellows were after her. Even when she became pregnant
and married Walter, somehow she still seemed innocent.

On the other hand, she, Esther, had always been too efficient. She had
always done what was expected of her, even at the age of fourteen when
she was hired out to an elderly couple on a neighbouring farm. All her
money, fifty cents a day, she handed over to her mother on Sundays, her
afternoon off. Her brother would come for her with the wagon and take
her home to help catch up with the mending and scrubbing, to help make
Sunday dinner. Not that Esther had ever minded. On the contrary; for
her mother's sake she would have done ten times as much work. She
blamed her parents for nothing.

Later, though, it did turn out that life was not always drudgery. That
was after the old couple retired to the city and Esther moved along with
them. When they died, through the minister of the church, she found
employment at another place. Sometime in there, she changed from a
hired girl to a live-in domestic.

Sometime, too, during those early years in the city, at one of the places where she worked, she started her secret scribblings. Was it loneliness? Some unfulfilled yearning? She did not know. She did not ask. It was as though some large force compelled her to jot down notes to herself in the evenings after the kitchen was scoured, the dishrag rinsed in bleach, and she was back in her room. Sometimes, she had to swing herself out of her warm bed, her feet onto the cold floor, and rummage for a stub of pencil and a scrap of paper. After a while she started keeping a pencil and paper beneath her pillow. Esther felt satisfied that, unlike other people, she had no illusions. What she kept hidden, to bring out and look at only when she was alone, was a harmless hobby.

She took a sip of coffee to settle her nerves. The coffee had no taste as far as she could tell. And she did not like the thick porcelain mugs Gertrude called cups. They were crude and ugly. In later years, in those last houses, Esther's lips became accustomed to fine china. Towards the end she worked in some pretty ritzy places, as she liked to tell Gertrude. She knew about serving food properly and speaking in a low voice.

Walter was sitting directly across the table from her. He was talking about what *he* had told the foreman he could do with the four day work week. Esther, resigned to watching Walter's long red face and his wisps of white hair that moved with his jaw, did not like the four day work week any more than he did. That was why he was at home on a Friday morning. Starting the day with Walter gave Esther indigestion. Not that she disliked him, exactly. But once, when he had been to the beer parlour after work, he called her "that skinny dried-up old maid sister of yours" to Gertrude. Esther had heard from her room. She prided herself that she did not hold grudges, and she hoped she was above minding what a silly old fool said when he was drunk. It was just that she felt better knowing he was safely down a sewer pipe or driving around in the city engineering truck.

"How d'y'want em?" Gertrude's girlish, high-pitched voice sliced across Walter's story and rang through the sound of her banging a pan onto the stove. Why Gertrude had to ask that question every morning, Esther would never know, since she always had boiled and they always had fried. But she realized that Gertrude was like that, talked just to hear herself, even though it was exhausting for people who had to listen.

Esther felt suddenly tired and oppressed. What was it? The sameness? The inevitability? She took a deep breath but could not fill her lungs. Her air came bang up against something solid and immovable. She pressed the bones of her chest with the outspread fingers of her hand. It's this house, she decided, so narrow, so close to the other houses, never any air in it or around it. For some reason, this made her think of Horowitz.

She was not against men, like some people, like Walter, thought. She had, at various times in her life, had men friends. One time there had been passion; afterwards she decided it had not been love. But that was something she did not allow herself to think about, because in the end it had been undignified, even shameful. But if a nice, refined gentleman came along, she would be more than willing. She would enjoy going out occasionally to a cafe for supper, to a band concert on a Sunday afternoon. She had always enjoyed playing whist. But there were simply no men like that here. Here there were only Walter and Horowitz.

The first time she saw Horowitz, he appeared as a dark figure, waiting in the shadows. Shortly after she came here to live she was walking in the evening with Gertrude. They walked past Horowitz's small frontyard. Up until then Esther was enjoying the walk immensely. That was before she knew what this neighbourhood was like, that many of the houses had been abandoned by their owners and neglected by their tenants. The ones with neatly clipped lawns and small flower gardens along their fronts were outnumbered and on the defense, obviously about to lose the battle of order and decency to future chaos.

Esther did not mind houses being small and plain, old and cramped together. Many old neighbourhoods were like that, and actually, she felt more comfortable around those houses than in the suburbs where everything was bare and made of plastic. And she liked the quiet people, most of them old, who puttered about in their yards with trowels and watering cans, the people who belonged to the neat houses. One evening she noticed an old couple kneeling together near a flower bed. This made her think of a painting she had seen once of people kneeling in a field at sunset, giving thanks after the day's labour.

Esther did not even mind poverty. At least she knew there was nothing to be ashamed of in it. Her mother had taught all of them that. Esther did not mind people who were poor as long as they were clean and respectable. It was the other ones, the young men with ratty long hair, dirty jeans, the children with that musty smell, the young woman who lived down the street. She had a big stomach and flapping rubber sandals and never seemed to comb her hair or go to the dentist. She was always screeching at her dirty, snivelly children who seemed to be going in and out of the doors and windows of their run-down house at all hours of the day and night. When the lights were on you could see through the window, straight through the living room into the back kitchen, see into the filth and clutter, see the beer bottles and overflowing ashtrays piled up on the kitchen table. These were the people that Esther could not help but despise, the ones who seemed to have lost respect for themselves as human beings, or maybe never had it in the first place. People without even the decency to pull their blinds and lower their windows on their depravity, who exhibited it on a stage for all the world to see.

Horowitz did not exhibit himself that way. He did not like to waste electricity. He preferred darkness. He had once told Walter, Walter was faithful in his reporting, that in the old country and later here during the early years, there was no electricity. When it was dark, it was dark. And unless he needed light for something specific, he did not bother with a lantern. He always sat in darkness to smoke his evening pipes. He had never learned to read the language of this country. "You don't need light for thinking," he had said to Walter. "It's all up here," he tapped his head, "like a picture show."

The evening of that walk had been warm, early autumn. The air was rose-coloured from dust and smoke and smelled of dry leaves. Horowitz's yard was patchy with crabgrass and weeds, bordered by a broken fence. Walking just in front of Gertrude and Esther was a young girl with fat thighs, her short skirt riding up on her legs. The women were half-way past the yard when they noticed Horowitz on his covered porch. His rocking chair was still, his body limp. His head, his eyes, were following the girl. Esther noticed the way he eased his trousers from his crotch. Even then, Gertrude called out good evening. Horowitz nodded. Then as they passed, Esther felt his eyes on her, first probing the spot between her shoulder blades, then lowering. She straightened her back, stiffened it, but that did not seem enough against him. Later, what she could not understand, could not explain, was that the feeling had been more than discomfort. She had actually felt threatened.

What she had seen and heard of him in the two years since that walk only confirmed her first opinion. He was a nasty, disgusting old man. And she said as much to Walter when Walter leered and made remarks like, "You should be nice to him, he's the kind to have a fortune hidden in the mattress." Then with a smirk, "But first you gotta get close to the mattress..." Often Walter said these things after he had ambled over to

Horowitz's shack, usually on a Saturday night, and then come home several hours later smelling like a brewery. The next day Walter would be full of insulting suggestions. Esther wondered if Horowitz planted them in Walter's feeble brain.

She supposed Horowitz would like someone like herself, someone to nurse him in his old age. Even if she was not as young as she used to be, even if sometimes now the curb edges caught her unaware, she was still in better condition than he was. But she had had enough of nursing people, and besides, she would never stoop so low as to have anything to do with someone like Horowitz.

Esther found herself breathing in short gasps. Her throat was tight. She sat up straighter and thrust back her shoulders and tried to expand her chest. It might help if Walter would stop talking for just one minute, she thought. He thinks he's so smart. He thinks he knows everything. But he doesn't know anything. Wouldn't he be shocked if he did know. Might be so shocked he'd shut up for a minute.

If he knew what she did in the privacy of her room. With a table knife slid between the wall and the door frame. He'd think I was crazy for sure, she decided. No danger of his ever finding out though, since he never read anything but the evening newspaper, and all he read of that was the page about the day's murders, robberies, and rapes. Anyway, she never sent anything in under her own name. If it ever got published it would be too embarrassing. She always used the name Tamar Ferouin. Many years ago she had seen that name in a novel she was reading. Esther thought then that it was an exquisite name, and she had never had any reason to change her opinion.

Thinking these things, her mind was carried. "Booth, looth," she mused. Walter's voice faded. The sound of Gertrude's pots and pans dimmed. One of the children spilled his milk but Esther did not notice. How about "lo' the"? she wondered. No she liked things to be neater than that. "Sooth, tooth...". That milk, she must get a cloth. Would Gertrude ever finish slamming things around? As for Walter, she knew he could go on forever.

Finally, finally, alone. Esther's room was small and square with one double window that faced out onto the front street. In it was a bed, a bureau, a trunk that doubled as a night table, a plain wooden chair. Through her life, as she had gone from house to house, she had tried to carry with her as few involvements as possible.

She sat down on the chair, before the window. The sun felt good on her legs, warm like a heating pad. Her legs ached sometimes now, not ached exactly, just felt weak and drained. "Yellow current of life," she thought, closing her eyes. "Warm streaming particles...". Through the open window she could hear street sounds, traffic, barking dogs, cries of children. She considered closing the window, but the air was so pleasant. She took a breath and started again. "I feel like a golden sponge," she thought, "filled with bubbles of weak...".

She could not think of the word she wanted. She remembered her dictionary, a small one she kept hidden because she knew Gertrude sometimes came into her room when she was not in it. She opened her eyes and turned her head sharply towards a place on the mattress. Was it still there? Would Gertrude, someone, have taken it? Of course not. She was becoming foolish, a foolish old woman. She thought of Horowitz's mattress, of his hidden gold which, of course, did not exist except in Walter's greedy imagination.

No, she squeezed her eyes tight. She would not let herself think these things, think about Horowitz and Walter during these precious moments she had set aside for her work. It was sacrilege to think of such things, those men, this place, during this special time. But how could she help it? There, now, were the voices, intruding, Gertrude and Walter having one of their several daily spats. How those two could have lived together all these years, could live together now, Esther did not know. People who fought like that, said such things to each other, terrible things, how could they forget all about it a few minutes later and go on as though nothing had happened? And the silly thing was, the fights were always over nothing. Like now—the walls in the house were so thin Esther could hear nearly every word—they were shouting about Walter's collection of burnt-out fuses and Gertrude's collection of old movie magazines. And, in addition to them, there were the children, the two youngest who did not go to school. They also had their rows, and besides that, were as noisy in their playing as in their fighting. Esther allowed herself a moment of despair.

She opened her eyes and stared without seeing. She found herself thinking, I should clean it out. She was looking at the top of her bureau, at a small wooden barrel from her mother's kitchen, used then for tea, stuffed now with odds and ends, old letters, pens, paper clips, hairpins, needles, thread. On the bureau, too, were a few old pictures, one of her parents. They were standing before the farmhouse wearing their Sunday best. Her mother's large-knuckled hands hung heavily, gracelessly, down. Those hands, always red, the skin always split, always had garden dirt in the torn cuticles. Another picture of her mother flashed into Esther's mind. She was standing in front of the iron stove, stirring something in a big black pot while a mess of ragged children scampered about her staunch thighs and her wide ugly bare feet.

No. No. Esther shook her head as though to clear it. Freedom, she thought. Freedom and beauty which the soul may feel, perfect and whole. Perhaps that was why the memory of gulls was so meaningful. Soaring freedom. Yes, she could write about that.

Esther tried to keep from doing it, but it was as though a strong hand pushed her head down so that she was looking at her own feet. While she had never liked her looks, her body or her face, she had learned to ignore them. But she had never learned to ignore her feet. Her feet were the only thing that in all those grand houses had always given her away. She had her mother's feet, flat and shapeless. As a girl she had lain awake nights wondering how she was ever going to get through life with such feet. Yet here she was. She had made it.

Of course she had made it. Thanks to no one but herself. Thanks to her own effort. She had always been a good worker and no trouble, and the only reasons she was ever let go were when people moved or died. Even when they moved they sometimes took her with them. Once, the last place, where she was more like a paid companion, the people took her with them on a yacht for a three-month cruise. All in all, she thought she had pretty good memories, but she especially liked to remember the yacht. Yes, she had made it. Still she had always felt handicapped and now sometimes found herself wondering what sort of life she might have had if she had been born different, under different circumstances, to city people, established people.

Esther looked through the window, at the sky, flawless blue. She looked through the branches of the poplar that filled the front yard, that sucked all the good from the earth so that nothing else would grow for several feet in any direction, so that the grass was always only a scab on the dirt. And in spite of the tree's efforts, its instinct to grab everything, all the earth's nutrients, for itself, its branches were spindly, its leaves sparse, pitted and deformed by insects.

Suddenly, as though stuck by a pin, Esther sat up straight. Her body became rigid with determination. To work, to work, she scolded herself.

Enough of this laziness, this wool gathering. She must not let her mind start drifting like that. Those gulls, now, the ones she had seen from the yacht, soaring over the choppy waves or the calm stillness. True, when you saw them up close, like on the rail, they were dumpy and clumsy looking. But in the air they became beautiful. Graceful. What were some of the words she could use—"web-toed, aquatic, heavy, awkward"? But those were not poetic words. She remembered how those birds had eaten, had survived on, garbage thrown off the boat. They were scavengers. She shuddered. She wondered about whales. Whales might be better. She recalled seeing three of them together once, racing and frolicking. The way they had dived into the waves! The way the sun had made their wet backs glisten! How could she work that up?

Poised, ready to leap, Esther's mind was disturbed again, this time by the creaking of the stairs and footsteps shuffling in the hallway outside her door. Automatically, her eyes slid to the mattress.

"Esther?" It was Gertrude.

"Yes?"

"Me 'n Walter are goin shopping. You wanta come?"

No, she did not want to come. She wanted to stay home and get something done. But she would go down to see them out and to lock the door after them.

She stood on the back porch and watched them leave, each carrying a child. As they walked along the path to the garage, Gertrude pressed her body against Walter. He accepted her naturally. For him she was expected, perhaps even inevitable. Esther looked quickly away.

She watched Walter's car until it disappeared. At the same time she saw Horowitz, his bag full now, walking his slow walk. As the car passed him, he stopped and held up a hand. Then he turned his head and looked toward where Esther stood alone on the step. She went inside, closed the door firmly after herself, pushed in the lock. She stood without moving, her hand on the doorknob. In a few moments she heard what she was waiting for, someone outside on the porch. She heard the heave of a heavy weight up the steep narrow steps, the rasping of breath drawn in a throat. Then the knock came, three solid raps with the knuckles of a hand, a man's hand, not as strong perhaps as it used to be, but still strong, stronger than her hand.

I don't have to answer, she thought. I don't have to open this door. The room was suddenly hot, stifling. The clock ticked on the wall. She could scarcely hear it for the noise of her heart. She felt that surely Horowitz could hear her heart through the door. He would know she was standing there, that she was hiding, that she was afraid. She saw the absurdity of the situation. She was an old woman, no longer attractive to anyone. Likely all Horowitz wanted was to borrow something, Walter's gardening tools. She forced herself to open the door.

His face startled her. She didn't expect it to be so close. She had never really seen it before; she had always looked somewhere else. Now she saw pitted coarse skin and small purple veins running like threads beneath. There was something about his mouth, something violent. His teeth...

"Good day, lady." His voice was harsh and rusty. Nodding his head, he lifted his cap and bowed slightly.

Esther tightened her lips. She looked down. The bag of bottles was on the porch, at his feet. His boots were cracked; his trousers were baggy. She tried not to inhale.

"Excuse me please," he continued. "But I been thinking. I'm all alone, see. You, you're all alone, right? I got that house there. All paid for. I got my pension. I do all right. You'd be surprised, too, how much them bottles bring in." He gestured.

Walter, thought Esther. Walter put him up to this. During one of their drunken orgies. Maybe, even, there was money bet on it. It's their joke, she thought, or maybe not a joke. Walter never did want me here. It was Gertrude made him take me in. "Don't..." She raised a hand to protect herself. She backed away. Her heart beat in ragged, irregular strokes.

Horowitz took a step forward. He was in the house. "But it's lonely, y'know. An I miss the cooking. So I got to thinking. Two old guys like you'n me... They tell me you come from a farm, too, a long time ago, but... like, the way I figure, we're the same, you'n me..."

"No...no..." Esther backed up until she felt the corner of the kitchen counter in the small of her back. As she retreated, Horowitz advanced, so that he was standing close over her. His body, his smell, was all around her. His breath was on her face. He was standing so close she could not lower her head. She was forced to look at his face, at his eyes. What she saw there was recognition, instant and shocking. It was then that her heart seemed to burst. Because of the rush of sound in her ears, she could not hear. Because of the blackness, she could not see. Pain, at first soft and large, floated towards her until it was right on top of her. Then it bore her down with its weight. She reeled against something, felt hands reach for her. She wanted to hold onto something, but there was only Horowitz.

When she came home from the hospital, she spent most of her time upstairs, on her bed, making her way down slowly, like a child, one step at a time, for meals. Gertrude wanted to make a bed for her on the living room couch, but she said no, she did not want to be that much trouble. She knew she could not take such a constant dose of Walter and the children. And she realized, to be fair, that they did not want to see that much of her, either. Anyway, it would not be forever. Against Gertrude's protests (Walter had said nothing, had sat silently looking into the distance out of the hospital window), Esther had put her name in for a room in a government-subsidized nursing home. But the list was long, the list of other people like herself, people who could no longer take care of themselves.

Gertrude helped her dress in the morning and undress at night. Esther's right side did not work the way it should. When she first woke up in the hospital her arms were crossed and lying in a heap on top of her body. She could not feel them, feel anything. She could not remember anything, even Horowitz at first. But after a while some feeling had seeped back in, into her arms and legs, into her brain, although now her body would not always obey her brain's commands, and there were shadows around edges. And never since that day in the hospital when she asked the nurse for a mirror, never did she look in mirrors.

She could not sew, could not work with her hands; she could not read for long. At mealtimes she caught the children staring at her in fascination, staring at the side of her mouth. But worst of all, she could not think, at least not consistently, not coherently. She had not known that such things could ever happen to her.

On a day in late summer she was lying on her bed and a light tapping sound came at the window. She only had to raise her head to see. It was a branch of the poplar, and she thought how the ragged leaves were like old lace. "Lace-leaf," she thought. She liked the sound of that and wondered if it was a real word. "Lattice-leaf," she thought and liked that even better. For the first time since what everyone called her 'accident,' she remembered her dictionary. She wondered if it was still beneath the mattress. Maybe Gertrude had found it when she changed the bedding. Slowly, Esther moved her body until she was standing on the floor. Leaning on the bed for support, she knelt. Sliding her good hand between mattress and spring, she found what she was looking for.

She settled herself back on the bed and opened the book. She forced her eyes down the black columns of words until she found it. She struck her finger at the place. *Lattice-leaf, a submerged aquatic plant of Madagascar, broad leaves consist only of veins which float just beneath the surface, tiny white flowers.* She set the dictionary on top of her trunk. It did not matter any more if Gertrude saw it. She would tell Gertrude to give it to the children. Maybe they could use it in school. Exhausted, Esther lay back against the pillow. She opened her mouth. It felt frozen, as if she had been to the dentist. Still, she willed her lips to say it one time. "Madagascar," she whispered, lingering over each syllable.

## The Eternal Bachelor

Arnold heard music, piano music, light and lovely. Laurel was playing again, one tune after another, as though she would never stop. He stood beside her, at her shoulder. He felt light as the music. His hand reached out. The cloth of her dress was thin. He could feel her small bones, her warm flesh. He felt her small flutterings of life.

"Northern," said Meg, clamping her jaw square.

"Baltimore," said Arnold, just as emphatically.

"You can't say that," said Meg. "You have to see its eye."

The oriole's head was turned away from them. It was singing, perched on a leafy branch outside the picture window of Arnold's third-floor apartment.

"No, I don't," said Arnold. "It doesn't have a white patch on the wing."

"It's the light," said Meg. "Go get your glasses. You can't see anything without your glasses anyway."

Arnold opened his mouth to say something equally rude, but then he didn't want to spoil the bird's singing. As though its life depends on it, he thought. And how can such a glorious sound come out of that tiny thing? And without thought or effort? It transports you, he marvelled. It simply transports you.

"Close your mouth or you're going to catch flies," Meg said.

Arnold closed his mouth quickly, without thinking. Then he wished he had kept it open just long enough so Meg would know she couldn't boss him around. He supposed Meg couldn't help it. She was a nurse, a private nurse now, and had been bossing people around for thirty years. Still, he thought, even if she was good for him, as everybody said, he would never have married anyone like Meg. "I don't know why you don't marry that woman and get it over with," his mother used to say. But his taste ran to dainty women, fragile women. And he saw nothing wrong with a bit of paint and polish. Meg, standing beside him in her grey skirt and jacket, her sensible shoes, was as solid and implacable as a warden. He couldn't imagine two more different women than Meg and Laurel.

The bird flew off and Meg turned back into the room. Alone at the window, Arnold let himself go into a trance. There was something about the poplar tree. Maybe it was the new green of the leaves, or the way they shimmered. He saw a boy in the tree. It was himself. He had just climbed out the front bedroom window at the old house, onto the verandah roof and into the tree. He wasn't sure whether he was Tarzan or Errol Flynn. Whichever, he was about to leap onto the ground. But there was his grandmother, hands on hips, waiting for him below. "Oh shu! You great lunk of a thing you. What're you doing there now, clammerin all over the roof and waking up your mother? Get away with you there."

"We're going to be late," Meg called from the door. "It's already seven."

Arnold checked the stove, the back lock, and the lights. He left two lights on, in strategic locations, so burglars would think he was home. His silent watcher approved these brisk, efficient movements, for whether it was setting his table, running laps at his gym, or computing columns of figures at his office, he always had this sense of audience and performance.

But then he couldn't find his glasses. He knew he had them on when he came home from work. He couldn't drive without them. As he quickly retraced his steps, bathroom, bedroom, Meg said if he wasn't so vain and would keep them on his face, he wouldn't always be losing them.

"I can't keep them on my face," he called from his kitchen. Nothing here; the counters were clear. The round table by the window was as it should be – in the centre, salt, pepper, a green plastic owl stuffed with paper napkins.

"I wouldn't be able to see if I did," he called. "It's distance I can't see." He had told her this a hundred times, but she refused to believe it.

Meg spotted the glasses on the arm of the chesterfield where he had sat to drink his one cup of decaffeinated coffee. While he locked the door, she pressed the elevator button. He always took the stairs. This was part of his fitness routine, part of the reason he was still lean and wiry and proud of it. Meg always said she was fit enough. They met at the bottom. His spry dance darted around her paced steps to open the outside door.

They were on their way to a piano recital. It was a June evening, still day-bright, the air warm and fragrant. As they walked across the thick springy grass between sidewalk and car, Arnold thought, *What is so rare as a day in June?*

"Did you remember the tickets?" asked Meg.

Arnold enjoyed the recital immensely. He liked all music, but he especially liked piano music. This was because of Laurel. When he listened to piano music he always closed his eyes and saw her. The first time, he was peeking through the curtain of his room. She was out on her back step, in her bathrobe, taking in the milk bottles. Her dark hair was tousled, her robe loose at the top. She was not aware of watching eyes; she was completely abandoned.

She was in her kitchen. She and his mother were drinking tea and smoking cigarettes while he sat cross-legged on the floor entertaining Tony. Tony was little more than a year and he was thirteen, but he didn't mind. It gave him a chance to see what went on at Laurel's and why his grandmother disapproved of her. As he built great pyramids of blocks for Tony to knock down, he watched Laurel's slim fingers, the way they tapered at the tips. No one in his family had fingers like that.

She was in his grandparents' living room, sitting on the sofa, the one that was now in his living room. Her face was greenish-white, and all she did was stare, until she saw the piano.

Arnold deposited Meg in front of the San Palito Towers. She wondered if he wanted to come in for something to drink. She had ginger ale or tea. He said no, he was tired after the week's work. She said who was he trying to kid, no one works at the City. He said the finance department did.

It was true he was tired, but besides that, recitals always put him in a certain mood which did not include Meg. As he watched her make her way up the walk and into the glass-walled foyer, he had a brief pang of guilt. She doesn't mind, he told himself. One thing about Meg, he never had to worry about her being lonely or having her feelings hurt. She was too self-reliant for that.

At home, he made himself a cup of tea. He drank it standing before his kitchen window. As his eyes travelled beyond the white wooden balcony and stairs, they saw the parking lot below become a back garden of huge leaves and tangled vines. His mother was making her way through the shadows, through the wire gate and across the lane. He watched until she disappeared into the rectangle of light that was Laurel's open door, then he climbed into his bed, folded his hands across his chest and strained his ears to hear the kitchen door below, signalling her return. Usually, he couldn't stay awake that long. He fell asleep imagining the two women talking into the night. He heard their whispers and wondered about their secrets. In the same room, in another bed, his father was dying. He always assumed then that his father was asleep those nights. But now he often wondered if perhaps he, too, had been staring into the darkness, waiting.

But that was on his mother's night off. The other six nights a week, she made up her lunch, had a snack, and went off to mend airplane wings. People said she was working for the war effort, but he knew that finances were low, that was why they were living with his father's parents, and that she was working for their effort, for him and his father. On those nights, he listened for the streetcar, a block over, that took her away. He pictured her stepping up, putting her ticket into the glass, taking a seat. As the streetcar jerked to a start, she settled herself sleepily against a window. Downtown, there was a special bus that took her to the airport, to where there were people, people who spoke and laughed.

Compared to night, day was boring. There was the piano, but its lid was always closed. No one ever played it, except Laurel that time. The only music in his life were hymns at church on Sunday.

The piano music was kept in a tapestry-covered wooden box tied around with thick cord. Once, he opened this box and was nearly smothered by the smell of dry old paper. He lifted his eyes to the photographs, yellow and faded, on top of the piano, aunts and uncles and cousins of his grandparents. He had never seen any of them. They might have all been dead. But their eyes were alive, accusing him. Dark coats hanging on a rack near the door shifted in disapproval. Quickly, he shut the lid and put everything together exactly as it had been.

Outside, there was only one other boy his age, a boy who for some unknown reason singled Arnold out as the object of a peculiar hatred. Whatever the motive, this boy would lie in wait for him to step out of his yard, then pelt him with rocks.

Until his grandmother put a stop to it, there was the escape game, from window to roof to tree. His mother often slept on the verandah, at one end screened with canvas and mosquito netting, especially when the days were hot. Her being there made the game more challenging. The object was to escape without waking her up. Once on the ground, he crept up the verandah steps, crossed the creaky floorboards, and pushed aside the netting. He liked catching her that way. She looked younger when she slept, a real picture, her face relaxed, smooth. But it was more than that. He couldn't exactly describe it, but when she was sleeping she was turned inward on herself, disconnected to the world. He didn't want to wake her up, because then her face changed. She suddenly looked old and tired. She scolded him. He didn't blame her. He knew that her life was a series of desperations.

"Why don't you get rid of that old piano," Meg said. "It just clutters up the place."

"All those corners and curls," Bertha said. "You can't dust. Even the vacuum can't get into those crevices."

"It's not as though you can play it," Frank said.

It was bridge night. For twenty years the four of them had been meeting like this. Tonight it was Arnold's turn to host. They were onto the eats, tuna buns he had wrapped in foil and heated in the oven. Now Bertha was telling him what he needed was a kitchen like Meg's, which was hardly a kitchen at all. And Frank was going on about the view at Meg's. As far as Arnold was concerned, Meg's view was a panorama of other high rises, and he would choke in her kitchen. No thanks, he thought. Not that he cared, if that was the way other people wanted to live. But why couldn't they leave him alone?

"The Arms suits me fine," he said.

"Oh, it's so shabby," said Meg. "All these things built in the late forties, right after the war. They depress me. I don't know why you want to remind yourself of that time. You had to wait a month for a phone."

"Lucky if you got one in a month," said Frank.

"At least I don't have to go outside to turn around," said Arnold.

"He doesn't want to leave his old things," said Meg.

"No sense keeping old things," said Frank. "What's the use of old things?"

"They belonged to my grandparents," Arnold reminded them. He patted the arm of his chair. "And besides, they don't make stuff like this nowadays."

"Just as well," said Bertha. "Who'd want things that last forever? Then you could never get new."

"It's all so dark," Meg accused. "And heavy."

Arnold let them talk. They had been at him like this for the last two years, since his mother died. Up until then, she had lived with him. Before she died, they used to tell him that was why he never married. He didn't have to. She did everything for him. This was proof that they knew nothing about him.

"But the cleaning," Bertha was saying. "Think how you could cut down on the cleaning."

"I don't know why you don't get someone in to do the cleaning," Frank said. "You wouldn't catch me cleaning."

"Oh, don't try to tell him," Meg said. "He doesn't trust his old things to strangers."

What do they know about me? thought Arnold. The truth was he liked cleaning. Often, when he was vacuuming, he would lift up the lid of the piano and strike a few notes. That was enough to bring it all back, as though the intervening years did not exist. Laurel was with him again.

When he was brushing his teeth, he thought, what does anybody really know about anybody else? The people we never see are sometimes the people we know best. Laurel had moved away at the end of that summer. He had not seen her for more than forty years. Yet he knew her as well as he knew himself. He knew every detail about her. He saw her hair falling forward around her face. He heard her voice, full of life.

"What is it this time?" she said to his mother who had just said, "Is she ever on her high horse." It was something about his grandmother, something about the war, one of his uncles who was in a minesweeper, something about his mother laughing at the funnies when there was nothing to laugh about in this world. He was not really listening. He was watching Laurel's high heels, her silk stockings, her red lipstick.

On the table was a glass ashtray. Between the faces of the two women, smoke curled upwards. Laurel offered the pack to his mother, but she said no thanks, "She'll smell it on my breath." Some days his mother either took the chance or didn't care. But this day she was cautious and upset. "Do we all have to stop living?" her voice suddenly burst out on a high pitch.

Tony started crying and Laurel took him up on her knee. "Run'n get me his soother, will you?" she said, turning her marvelous wide smile on him. "It's in the bedroom, just down the hall there."

There wasn't much furniture in the room, a bed, a dresser, a crib, but everything was neatly arranged. On the dresser was the teething ring, faded blue, lying just before a picture of a young man in uniform with his arm around Laurel. They were smiling at the camera. They seemed young. That was when Arnold thought how Laurel was really only a girl, not much older than he.

Laurel. The name leaped off the page. It was an unusual name. Arnold's eyes darted over the column, searching for details. Not Hendricks. The age, though. She would be sixty-one. And survived by sons, daughters, the oldest Anthony James. That would be little Tony. She must have remarried. Of course she would have remarried, a young beautiful woman like her. It was only right that she should have remarried, should have had someone to look out for her, take care of her.

Arnold dropped the newspaper across his breakfast dishes. He was transported to the old house, the front room. It was evening. His grandparents and his mother were reading the newspaper. He was reading Dickens' *The Life of Our Lord*, a gift from his grandmother. Every hour on the hour his grandfather turned the radio on. Then the air became tense. At mention of certain strategic locations, his grandparents leaned forward and woe betide anyone who made the slightest noise or movement. He knew this was because his uncles were off fighting the war.

When the news was over, sometimes a few bars of music escaped from the box before his grandfather reached over from his armchair and clicked the button. Directly after the nine o'clock bulletin, the old man stood up, the signal for everyone else to do the same. He switched off all the lights. Arnold was sent to bed. The adults went into the kitchen to prepare things for the next day, his grandmother to soak the porridge, his mother to get ready for work.

Near the end of that summer, one evening was different. They were sitting reading in the living room as usual, but then a knock came at the back door. It was a terrible moment. Fear etched every face in that room. Arnold could see that. It was a time of death, and no family was safe.

It turned out that the death was connected to Laurel. Her husband. She stood in the open door, clutching Tony in her arms. His mother took Tony and got Laurel into the living room. They couldn't get her to speak. For the longest while she sat there staring into space. Then she seemed to become aware of the piano. She got up slowly, went over to it, and lifted the lid. She sat down and started to play, without sheet music, mournful tunes at first, but then the rhythm changed into something lively. It made him think of those snatches of music on the radio. She played and played, one tune after another, as though she had to, as though she dare not stop.

That was when he went and stood beside her. And after a moment, she looked up at him. Her face was dry and hot looking. "Come on. Sing," she said.

He stood there, stricken. He did not know how to sing.

Arnold's mother remembered the words. She joined them at the piano. The two women sang together as loud as they could. They almost shouted. The room seemed to burst. He would never forget.

Arnold wished now that he had discussed that evening with his mother before she died. There were things he would never know. He wondered what his grandparents had thought. He wondered what mystery of his mother's life allowed her to know such songs. And his ghost of a father, upstairs. Had he heard? What had he thought? Had he ever known such songs? Now he wished he had asked her whatever had become of Laurel. Well, it was too late. They were all dead. Now all the people who had really known him were dead.

Arnold came back to his newspaper. He wished he could turn the clock back five minutes and skip the obituaries this morning. He thought how he had just about gotten through his whole life without knowing.

It was Saturday. On weekends Arnold always enjoyed lingering over his breakfast and the paper. Then, he would get busy. Sundays it was a brisk walk, Saturdays his housecleaning. This morning he sat longer than usual, staring at the print. After awhile, he supposed he should get moving. He took the vacuum out of the cupboard. He kept stopping, as though uncertain about what to do next.

He sat down on the piano stool and lifted the lid. He struck a few keys. He played the C scale and chord. The notes quivered in the air, harsh and discordant, horribly distorted. Why had he not realized before that the piano was so out of tune. Even then, when Laurel played it, it must have already been out of tune. He wondered if his friends were right.

The funeral was Monday. He had to go, he couldn't help himself. Afterwards, he was surprised that he had felt no premonition of disaster. Looking down at the bloated colourless figure nestled in its satin bed, he wondered that she could have changed so radically.

There was a man shaking hands with everyone. He turned out to be the right person. "I used to keep you amused," Arnold explained. "Babysit, I guess you'd call it."

The man was not unfriendly, simply detached. "I'm sorry I don't remember..."

"You were a baby," said Arnold. "You couldn't possibly remember."

They spoke a few minutes longer. Laurel had died of a stroke, high blood pressure. She had been on medication for some years. Looking at the face of this man in his early forties, Arnold could not recall his other face. Every time he tried to think of little Tony, Anthony Hendricks intervened.

That week he missed one of his fitness classes. He just didn't feel up to it. He tried to get out of bridge. "I think I'm coming down with something," he said, "a cold maybe, the flu."

"Doesn't do you any good to stay at home feeling sorry for yourself," Meg said over the phone. "We won't let you breathe on us. And would you pick up a carton of coffee cream on the way over?"

They knew something was wrong with him. They thought it was his work. "You always liked a challenge," said Frank. "You must be getting old."

Arnold supposed Frank was right. He was getting old, and he may as well admit it. He gave up his hair conditioner. He started wearing his glasses all the time. He found it more and more difficult to drag himself out to the gym. He was often stiff. When he stood up it took him a moment to straighten his back. Meg commented. "It's only natural," he said. "Next month I turn fifty-six."

He took to long periods of sitting. When he went for a walk, he would find a bench and stare at the river, the grass, whatever fell into his line of vision. One day he thought, what does it matter whether I sit here or stand or walk. There is no one to see me. There was no one to admire his still flat belly, his still thick hair, his agile step.

Another day, he came to the sudden realization that Laurel had never seen him. Because he had seen her so vividly, he had assumed that she saw him. He had been performing all his life for someone who was not there.

It's over, he thought. In his apartment he sat for hours, a book open on his lap, without turning a page. His mind was a blank. He couldn't remember anything any more. When he tried to think about Laurel, she flickered on and off in his brain. He tried to touch her but he could not feel. He tried to listen to the music but he could not hear.

For his vacation that year, he and Meg had planned to drive to the Coast. He begged off. She went by herself on the bus. She came back and told him she had a great time. He spent the three weeks in his apartment, shuffling from the back window to the front window. He turned on the TV but he could not concentrate on the story or what the people were saying. He sat in front of the set for hours, watching the movement on the screen. He turned off the TV and went to bed. He climbed between his sheets. They felt cold. His skin flinched.

For three weeks he didn't shave. He wore the same clothes every day. He ate anything, whatever was easiest, cold canned spaghetti, half-baked frozen french fries. He knew he should clean up the place, but he didn't have the energy. The garbage bags piled up at the door. One morning he looked down and noticed something green and hairy growing on top of tea bags and soggy bread scraps. He stared at it for a long time. He couldn't decide what to do about it.

He knew he was finished, but in September he realized that even if he was finished, he had approximately twenty years to go. The conditions of life had changed, that was all. There was nothing he could do about it. He must simply go on. He must go to work each day. He must go through the motions. Nothing specific happened to make him come to this realization. It just occurred to him.

His friends thought he was back, or nearly back, to normal. The pressure was off at the office, the flu symptoms gone. His looks had changed. He knew they had changed. Nothing you could put your finger on, not thinner, not more lines, something less robust perhaps, something diminished, some permanent mark of experience, some boundary crossed to another point of no return. Well, they were all changed. Arnold looked at their faces. He scarcely recognized them. The set of Meg's jaw was becoming more stubborn and unyielding every year. Her hands were getting larger as arthritis set in. And Bertha, the way she stuffed her mouth with those pinwheel sandwiches she had concocted. She looked like pink cream cheese. And Frank, his hair was thin, almost white. Brown splotches were spreading on his face and hands.

He thought of Laurel, not in the old way, but in the new way, as a name, a word in his mind. What had happened was not her fault. She was only human. A human being could not stay in the state of an open wound. He had put too great a burden on her, to carry his imaginative life for so many years simply because at a particular moment, perhaps the most vulnerable moment of her life, he had seen her, or thought he had.

Still, he thought, I did know her for that moment. He was sure of it. No one had known her as he had. Maybe to know another person completely for one moment was all one could expect of life.

He thought of the boy who had listened to voices in the night through floors and walls, a boy who had looked for light through windows and cracks. That boy had felt that adults were luckier than children and that when he was an adult he would suddenly be happy. He had known that adults could be lonely too, but they had ways of escaping. They were in control of their loneliness. Adults were free to go to where there were voices and light. Except for his father, but that had been a special case, much like his own. He knew now that such freedom was an illusion and that for it he had given up everything, what most people called life. Still, he would not have done it any other way. He had been happy! What do they know? he thought fiercely. Any of them? What do they know? He had no regrets. He had had a good life. Surely, with Laurel, no one had been happier than he.

## Ordinary Murders

Mrs. Harris could have killed Allan but then a knock came from the back porch. They were at the face-off, in a narrow space between sink and cupboard, over a bowl of cornflakes in Allan's hand.

The door opening and Tom's voice saved them. "Hi, anybody home?"

Mrs. Harris turned and put on her other face. "Of course. Of course we're home! Where else would we be?" As she propelled herself forward, she tried to recall her last words, Allan's last words. How loud had their voices been?

She kissed Carol and lifted Normie out of her arms. She kissed Tom. She prided herself that after the dust settled she had accepted Tom right into the family and that he, along with her own, called her Mom.

Tom set down a folded playpen and stroller. He straightened and turned. "I'll be back," he said over his shoulder, his face toward them, his baseball cap pushed back on his black curly hair, his dark eyes smiling on them all.

Mrs. Harris thought how even if Tom wasn't long on brains, he was certainly cheerful. And sincere. She had to give him that.

She jostled her grandson up and down. "Hello 'ittle man, howsa 'ittle man," she cooed. He hung limply in her arms, against her bony chest.

"He was asleep in the car," explained Carol. "He's not quite awake yet." Then, seeing the direction of her mother's gaze, toward the tops of Normie's bare legs, "It's the heat. They all have it. It's only normal in this heat."

"Those girls in those day cares," said Mrs. Harris, "they're so busy. It's not their fault."

"It's not the day care. It's just this heat."

"That's what I mean. Please don't misunderstand me. I'm sure they all have that diaper rash. All of them in that day care."

She set Normie down in the old high chair. She straightened, turning at the same time, and caught a look between Carol and Allan. Allan was shaking his head. Mrs. Harris's pale eyes narrowed. "What are you two up to this time?" she asked.

"Nothing."

"Whaddayamean?"

"Just like when you were kids. Planning some devilment. Oh well, don't tell me. You never did. Tell me anything. But I always found out in the end."

She stood back and studied Normie. "What are those blue smudges under his eyes?" she said. "And he looks so white. Have you had his blood checked lately?"

Normie looked up at them, his forehead worried with fine creases.

"He's fine," said Carol. "It's just this heat. Is it ever gonna let up?" She dropped her bag heavily onto the floor and sank into a chair. She pushed a piece of blonde hair behind her ear.

"Nope," said Allan. "They say it's breaking all records for August. The radio."

"The worst is there's no air," said Mrs. Harris, clutching her throat. "They say it's the forest fires near the mountains. That's why everything's so hazy. The smoke comes into the house. Even if you close the windows. It gets in through the cracks. These old houses..."

"I hope it's cool at the beach," said Carol.

"It's bound to be cooler than this," said Mrs. Harris. "With the water and all. Water always has a cooling effect. Even if it is just in your head."

Tom returned carrying a diaper bag and a walker. "Did I forget anything?" he said and sat down.

"Looks like you're gettin' ready for a siege," said Allan as though he disapproved.

"That's what it's like," said Mrs. Harris. "Once you start carrying things, there's no end to it. One thing just leads to another." She stood, almost invisible in the pale light of the window behind her, and looked at the pile of things on the floor beside Carol.

"We should go," said Carol, rousing herself.

"You can't go," said Mrs. Harris, coming to life, "without a cup of coffee." Her voice was triumphant. "I just managed to save us some cream." She didn't look at Allan.

That was how it started, Allan stabbing his spoon into his cornflakes and muttering, "I don't know why in hell you hafta get this crap for anyway," meaning the skim milk.

But before that, he opened the fridge and reached for the cream. She said, "That's for the coffee when they get here." That set him off, but she showed remarkable control. She could have said a lot of things, like, maybe when you pay your way around here you can expect cream. But she knew she must not let him start anything. She knew it was absolutely necessary for her to keep a grip on herself because it was turning out to be one of those days.

Actually, it started earlier. She had slept badly; she had a headache or, more accurately, an eye ache, as though her eyeballs had been bouncing around in her head all night. She knew this happened when you dreamed. It was like your eyes were up all night watching television. But you couldn't choose the channel. She would have preferred something cheerful like "The Waltons". Instead, she was tuned into "Twilight Zone". Last night she had dreamed of Carol, only it didn't look like Carol. In her dream Carol looked like one of those pictures you see of famine victims. It seemed to be after a war. There was a building, a shack with a long verandah, in ruins. There were large pits and depressions in the ground. Nothing grew in that place. Carol was disappearing, it wasn't clear how or where, only that she couldn't follow. She had to stay in this place. She didn't know why. There was no reason. But that was the way things were in dreams.

She couldn't remember when she had dreamed this. When she was suddenly awakened by the body bump-bumping down each step, was the dream in full swing then on her private screen? Or after that, when she was sinking and surfacing into and out of darkness for the rest of the night, did it happen then? Was it mixed in with his grumblings and cursings as he picked himself up and finally made his way back up the stairs and down the hall, past her door, Carol's old door, to his room? She remembered thanking heaven she was not in that room, not in that bed where she used to lie stiff and terrified waiting for that other body smelling of beer and stale cigarette smoke. After twenty-five years, she knew it so well, its weight sinking into the other half of the mattress, its groans and snores, its twitches and sodden sleep. At the same time, it was the body of a complete stranger.

"Horse piss," said Allan.

She looked at him, the way he stood, naked except for a pair of ragged faded jeans, leaning against the counter. She looked at his long blond hair which fell into his face and his full cheeks which gave him a permanent pout and wondered that he could be any child of hers. They all had those cheeks, all of the boys, just like their father. Carol was the only one like her, the only one with fine bones.

She opened her mouth. She closed it again, gulping air. She turned back to her sink full of dishes. She wouldn't start. Not this morning. She knew that if she started this morning something terrible would happen.

"There's never anything to eat around this house," Allan said through a mouthful of half-chewed cereal.

All I have to do, thought Mrs. Harris, is last until Carol gets here. Carol is on my side. I couldn't live if I lost Carol.

She wrung out her dishcloth and turned to wipe the counter. Allan stood in her way. She wiped the counter next to him and turned to wipe the counter opposite, but Allan was there again, pouring more milk into his cereal. She moved around him.

"A person could starve t'death around here," he said.

She heaved a deep breath into her narrow chest. But to breathe she had to straighten, and then she was looking through the window at the back yard and then the back yard came in at her through the window. Whenever she saw that mess, those scrap metal and rubber skeletons, she felt like saying and doing terrible things, things she could not help, things she would be sorry for later.

"Rick's mom makes them pancakes n' bacon Sunday morning," Allan said to her back.

Whenever she saw the dandelions spreading like beached starfish, the steps that needed painting, the honeysuckle beside the steps growing wild, spread all over, half-blocking the door so no one could get out or in, especially her with bags of groceries, enough groceries for five men, or at least males, which she didn't mind saying was one helluva lot of groceries, she was that exhausted she felt like lying right down and dying.

"She sets the table. With a tablecloth."

Mrs. Harris felt the skin around her eyes become rigid. She felt her face swell. She knew she shouldn't look, she should try to ignore that yard, but it was as if she was hypnotized and paralyzed at the same time.

"She puts flowers in a glass."

Control yourself, girl, she thought, or you'll never get through this day.

"That's one thing. Rick's mom talks to him."

She looked down into the sink. She watched the dishrag wipe quickly across a plate, the plate dip into rinse water and fit into a slot on the drying rack. Maybe if she concentrated on such details, the plates, not the yard, the plates and not her stringy arms and her hands that would never make it into one of those mother/daughter television ads, she would survive.

From upstairs came the sound of a mattress with a weight being shifted on it and feet on the floor. Mrs. Harris lifted her head.

"Some mother," said Allan. "You don't even know what a mother's supposed t'do."

"You're not going to get me going," said Mrs. Harris. "Not this morning."

"You're sad."

"I'm looking forward to this day. To babysitting my grandson. I don't often get the chance."

"So whose fault is that?"

She started humming to drown out Allan's voice. Besides, she knew her humming drove him up the wall.

"Nobody's but your own."

"When the roooooooooll is called up yoooooonder..." sang Mrs. Harris. Her voice was thin and shaky.

"If you hadn't had such a fit..."

"When the roooll is called..."

"When Carol was..."

"What about Carol?" Mrs. Harris demanded.

"What?"

"What did you just say about Carol?"

"Nothing."

"You distinctly said the name Carol. What did you say?"

"I can't remember. Jeez, you expect me to remember everything I say?"

"You know you said something about Carol!" She yelled. She knew she shouldn't but she couldn't help herself.

Allan looked at her with calm level eyes. Like an ant, she thought. Like I'm some ant he's frying with a magnifying glass.

"Jeez," he said, "you don't hafta get excited."

She turned abruptly to her pile of dirty dishes. She lifted a cup and saucer into the sink. She heard them rattle, and she all but dropped them into the water. Deliberately, slowly, she washed both cup and saucer. She forced her hands to stop shaking.

"Anyway," Allan said to her back, "it's not up to me to do her dirty work."

Mrs. Harris's shoulders tensed, but when her voice came it was light, almost airy. "Never mind," she said. "Carol will tell me. That is, if there's anything to tell."

Allan said nothing.

"She tells me everything."

Allan was silent.

"We've had our ups and downs, but we work things out."

Silence.

"That's the difference with someone you can talk to. Someone on your own level."

Allan snorted.

"Sometimes I think that Carol is the only person in my whole life I've been able to talk to. A person has to have at least one person to talk to. Otherwise you go crazy."

"You and your precious Carol."

"Two women in a house full of men. But we had, have, each other."

"How about that time with Tom? Some talking out that was."

"We never fought. We never had one fight."

"Only because Carol won't fight. At least not in the open. Instead she gets quieter and quieter. But it's fighting all the same. It's the worst kind. Isn't nothin' you can do with a person like that."

"It's true, she would never fight with you boys. You tried to make her fight. She just walked away. You boys had to go running after."

"She always had something we wanted. Because she was the oldest. She always had money from babysitting. She was the one who knew how to make them brownies, double chocolate..."

A crash came from somewhere upstairs. Curses trailed off into mumblings.

"The worst," said Allan, "was that time with Normie. I thought for sure that time she was never gonna speak to you again."

"She didn't understand." Mrs. Harris washed another dish and put it in the rack. "I was only thinking of her. She has a future. Why would she want to commit suicide?"

"Havin' a kid is hardly committing suicide."

"She has a career."

"So she gets to shove a bedpan under somebody's ass. Big deal."

"A nurse is a professional person."

"Your precious educated Carol."

"You're jealous. You're just jealous."

"Your precious educated career woman Carol."

"Just because you can't hold a job longer than three months."

"Clean up somebody's puke."

"Don't push me too far. Don't make me say things you'll regret."

"The fact of the matter is you don't know anything about Carol."

"You get more like your father every day," Mrs. Harris said.

"You're crazy!" shouted Allan, suddenly murderous. "You can't even see. I'm a lot taller than him."

"Tallness has nothing to do with it."

"Can you see me bald?" shouted Allan. He ran one hand through his hair. "With this hair?"

"You're exactly like your father," screamed Mrs. Harris with glee. She turned.

"You don't know nothin'!" shouted Allan. "Carol doesn't tell you nothin'! She knows you. She knows what you do with information!"

"It's already getting thin!" screeched Mrs. Harris. "On top!"

Allan opened his mouth for another assault but then the voice came. Tom's voice.

Mrs. Harris and Allan hung suspended. From somewhere in the house a toilet flushed. Water ran through a pipe along the ceiling, the wall, down to the basement.

"I wanted to have things nice," said Mrs. Harris, bringing the coffee to the table. "But Allan kept getting in my way."

"This is nice," said Tom. "Just dandy."

"I at least wanted to have those dishes done," she said. "But I never seem to get all the dishes done. If people would get up... imagine getting up at eleven."

"When I was young..." said Tom.

Mrs. Harris turned away and saw again the diaper bag, the walker, the stroller, the fold-up playpen. "I'm not going to fall into traps like you did," Carol had assured her, three years ago. "I'm different."

We're so much alike, thought Mrs. Harris. It isn't even funny. Except at her age I already had five kids. All I tried to do was make sure she had choices.

"It's not the end of the world," Carol had said on her wedding day. "I'm getting married, not dying."

"Boy, does that coffee ever hit the spot," said Carol.

"I suppose you've been up for hours," Mrs. Harris said. "Cooking and cleaning on your day off."

"No," said Carol. "Well. You know me. I don't sleep in any more anyway. Not with Normie." Then, quickly, "But I don't mind. I like mornings."

"You have to *try* and sleep in," said Mrs. Harris. "Especially when you're working that evening shift. Otherwise, you don't get your proper sleep."

"I'm fine," said Carol.

"Now don't go into one of your snits," said Mrs. Harris. "You know I'm only thinking of you. Why you won't let me take care of Normie, I'll never know. It would be absolutely no trouble at all, you know that."

"He likes going to day care. He has his friends..."

"He could stay here overnight sometimes." Carol sipped her coffee. "It's just that you look so tired these days. I don't like seeing my little girl look so tired."

"I don't feel the least bit tired. I feel great."

Tom broke it up. "How goes the battle?" he said to Allan.

"Oh," said Mrs. Harris. "I suppose you know. He's gone and quit another job."

Allan went to sit at the table across from Tom. "I'm not taking that kinda shit," he said, "from anybody."

"It's just about time, mister," Mrs. Harris's voice went a notch higher, "you learned you have to take some things in life you'd rather not take."

"Where is everyone?" Carol looked toward her mother.

"Oh, Calvin's over at a girlfriend's, as usual." Mrs. Harris brought more coffee, more cream. "And the others are out looking at used cars. I mean that's all we need around here, another wreck. Have you seen the back yard lately? There are three, no less than three, of them out there. It gets worse every summer. If your father would *do* something...

"And that honeysuckle," said Mrs. Harris, hitting her stride. "I don't know what I'm going to do if someone doesn't cut down that honeysuckle for me. Your father, another one of his bright ideas. He planted it. Nearly twenty years ago now, when we first moved here. Planted it and left it, like everything else, for me to take care of. That's a big job, you know, cutting down one of them things. It's a job for a man."

"You guys should do something about that honeysuckle for Mom," said Carol to Allan. "And take that stuff to the dump."

"I'm working on it," said Allan. "I bin busy."

"How can you say that?" shrieked Mrs. Harris.

"You might be able to get on at the hospital with me," Tom said.

Mrs. Harris thought how Tom really was a nice boy. And steady. She had to give him that. After all, the kids were doing all right. They just about had enough money for a down payment. A couple of times, on Sunday afternoons, they had taken her with them, out to one of those nice new developments, to look at the latest show homes. They did this, Carol and Tom, took her places. They thought she should get out more.

"You should take driving lessons," Carol often said. "Then you wouldn't be so tied down."

"Oh I will. I will. One of these days," she would answer. But then what good would that do anyway? Since she didn't have a car to drive.

Normie was contented, banging a toy against the tray of his chair. Carol was relaxed. Tom was leaning across the table talking to Allan. Mrs. Harris thought how they were a family, after all, in spite of everything.

She decided to feed them. "It's lunch time," she trilled, looking at the wall clock. "I'm just going to make us all a grilled cheese sandwich. I'm hungry myself. I was wondering why I felt a little shaky."

"We can grab something at McDonald's," said Tom, but Mrs. Harris was already pulling things out of cupboards, the electric frypan, the cord, knives for slicing. She pretended not to see Carol shrugging her shoulders at Tom.

"Restaurants are so expensive," she said. "Besides, that food's rotten, gives you gas and pimples."

She moved quickly between cupboard and fridge. She made herself slow down. She did not want to appear frantic. Against the murmur of their voices, she sliced cheese and buttered bread. She was almost humming, a real hum.

Mrs. Harris placed the sandwiches on the hot grill and turned. She noticed how Carol sat slouched, as though she didn't have the strength to sit up straight. Her rubber thongs were almost worn through. She had yellow callouses on her heels. Her hair looked like it hadn't been washed for a week. And there was Tom, in his pink T-shirt, looking great, and why not? Cock of the walk. But that's a man for you.

Well, she hoped Carol was satisfied. In the end, Carol always did exactly what she wanted. In the end she always used her final weapon to get her own way. And it had been Tom, she had to remember that, it had been Tom who had brought Carol around, persuaded her to forgive, that time. Forgive! Forgive what? Her concern? Her love? Carol's mistakes? That's what a mother does, thought Mrs. Harris, lets them forgive you for what they do.

"It's easy," Tom was saying. "Just go down and fill out an application."

"I dunno," Allan said. "Whadda they pay? I'm not workin' for no chicken shit."

Mrs. Harris pressed her lips together.

"Not that good to start," admitted Tom. "But it's not that hard or anything, just pushing those brooms and mops around. It's not exactly strenuous. And nobody hassles you much. As long as I've got 2E looking halfway decent nobody much gives a damn if I sit and have a cigarette or a cup of coffee with the guys. It's not that bad." He stretched and put his hands behind his head.

"Yeah?" Allan sounded mildly interested. Mrs. Harris began to hope.

"And the stories some of those old guys can tell," Tom continued. "They tell those stories over and over. Some of them go back to Dieppe and Normandy and places like that."

"If there's one thing I can't stand," said Allan, "it's old guys talking like that all the time."

Mrs. Harris could not take it, no matter how hard she tried. "Do you know how many jobs you've had in the past two years? Seven. Seven! Count them! That's what I have to do when I can't sleep at night. But, oh yes, you have to have the cream. But you're not willing to pay for the cream. Let somebody else pay for the cream!" She stopped. She turned away from them, from their alarmed faces, from Normie's frightened look.

Carol straightened, as though to stand. "Look, Mom," she said, "we don't have to go to the beach."

"I want you to go. I want you to have a day off." Even though it was you, she could have added, who got yourself into this mess in the first place.

"I don't need a day off," said Carol. "I have lots of days off." Her voice was suddenly detached. Be careful, Mrs. Harris told herself.

She turned to get the sandwiches. She was facing the window, the back yard. She turned to the table, platter in hand. She felt the beginning of a trembling at her lips. She pulled her mouth into a thin line. As she placed the platter of sandwiches in the middle of the table, she noted that her hand was almost steady.

She pushed the sandwiches at them, more coffee, cake, cookies she had made especially for Normie, his favourite, with chocolate chips but no nuts because they might get stuck in his throat.

She stood at the counter while she ate. She tried to make pleasant conversation. "Have you looked at any more houses?" she asked.

They were silent. They were chewing. "I remember you liked that model with the real fireplace," she kept on, taking a bite of grilled cheese.

Carol studied her sandwich.

"Not lately," Tom answered cheerfully enough. But there was something wrong. Mrs. Harris knew it. Because Carol acted that way again, as though she were under fire. Is that it? thought Mrs. Harris. Something wrong with the house plans then.

A rustling sound came from the stairs. In her mind, Mrs. Harris could see his slippers shuffle across the living room. He would be finding the Sunday paper now, on the coffee table that, try as she might, she could not keep uncluttered. He would be sitting himself down in his chair.

"Is that Grampa?" Tom said to Normie. "Can you say Grampa?"

"Maybe it's you who needs the day off," said Carol.

"Don't be silly," she said. "Normie and me are just going to have the best time." She went and tickled Normie under the chin. They would be looking for evidence.

Then it seemed so soon and they were leaving. Tom was standing at the door. Mrs. Harris was being sorry for the way she had flared up at Allan. She hoped she had not spoiled anybody's day.

Carol walked to the sink. She ran water from the tap over a cloth. She wrung out the cloth and walked back to Normie. She wiped chocolate from his face. A pregnant woman walks different, thought Mrs. Harris. Then Carol was bent over Normie. She was so thin, except for her stomach, her abdomen. When had she last seen Carol? A week ago for shopping. But then Carol had kept on her coat, her raincoat, a beige one. Before that, then? Another week when Carol and Tom had come for Sunday dinner. Carol had been wearing a loose dress, the one that Mrs. Harris had never liked.

Mrs. Harris jerked her eyes away. For a moment longer she held out against belief. Then she knew it was true. And Tom, standing there, smiling, leaning against the door, he knew. Of course, he knew. Was that all he was good for? Making babies? And Allan. Allan knew, too. They all knew. All of them, sooner or later, stuck a knife in your back. That's the thanks you got for lugging them around nine months inside you and forever after pushing and shoving them through life, to say nothing of the pain of birthing them and the hours spent trying to jam pureed spinach into them only to have it come back up plop on your shoulder. All the years of doing that, all the wasted years. What for?

Her eyes darted around the kitchen. How she hated this room. *He* had chosen the paint, pale blue. He had never asked what colour paint she wanted. He had simply come home with it one day, plopped the cans down in the middle of the kitchen floor, and left her to do something about them.

She felt like she was going down for the last time. She looked around for something to hold herself up with. Then she knew what she had to do. Her legs felt weak, but she made it to Carol and Normie.

"You're gonna have a real nice day with Granny," Carol was saying. Normie looked at Mrs. Harris. His eyes were large and trusting.

"I've been meaning to mention it to you," said Mrs. Harris, "for some time now." She touched Carol's arm, to give her support. She tried not to sound critical. "Have you noticed," she said, "the way his one eye turns in like that?"

Both women looked hard at Normie. He looked back at them. Two little worry lines formed between his eyes. "It looks all right to me," said Carol.

"Sometimes," said Mrs. Harris, "we don't notice things we don't want to see." There was a moment's silence. "You know dear, I don't want to interfere. But these things can be corrected so easily now, if you catch them. I hope you don't mind me mentioning it. I'm only thinking of what's best for you all."

"No," said Carol. "It's okay."

Normie, watching his mother closely, began to fuss.

"He'll settle down," said Mrs. Harris. "As soon as you leave." She turned to Normie. "Me'n you are gonna go over to the park for a little walk and have an ice cream," she said. "Now, how would you like that?"

But Carol said, "I don't like to leave him. He's going through a stage." She told Tom to put the things back in the car.

"What for?" said Tom.

"He'll be all right," said Mrs. Harris.

"What're y'doing?" Tom asked.

Carol didn't say anything. She was busy folding up the stroller.

"Tom, talk some sense into her," Mrs. Harris said.

"Carol..." Tom tried.

"Carol, don't be like that," Mrs. Harris pleaded. She looked again at Tom. Tom shrugged.

"Please leave him," said Mrs. Harris.

"It's getting late," said Carol. "We stayed too long."

"Don't punish me," said Mrs. Harris.

Carol said nothing.

"When will I see you?" asked Mrs. Harris, following Carol out the door. But Carol didn't hear. "I'll call tonight," she said to the side of Carol's face through the open car window.

Mrs. Harris stood on the sidewalk. She waved until the car disappeared and there was nothing left but silence settling down on the hot pavement. Still, she stood, squinting into the empty space where the car had been. It doesn't have to be the end, she thought.

She turned and looked in the other direction, down the dusty street of houses all like her own, two-storied houses on narrow lots, with patches of dried-up grass. Some of them had already been turned into rooming houses. She looked at the woody spaces in her caragana hedge, spaces knit by cobwebs and dirty bits of blown paper. She saw how the cement walkway was crumbling and how weeds and grass were growing into it and thought how she didn't have the strength to do anything about any of it. What was the use, she wondered. She had tried to make them a nice family, the kind you saw on TV.

She walked around to the back and saw the yard and the honeysuckle. As she went up the porch steps, the branches of the honeysuckle reached for her. She remembered how once, one of the boys, Allan, she was sure of it, during one of their rounds, had caught her arms and held them behind her back, how he had pretended it was a joke, how he had laughed at her struggles, how she had gone strange for an instant.

She ran up the last step. She rummaged around on the porch until she found what she knew was there some place, a pair of garden shears. She started hacking at the honeysuckle. She snapped viciously at each branch, cutting it, slicing it. Some of the branches tried to spring away. She made certain she got those ones. Some of them tried to strike her as they whipped forward. She made sure she got those ones, too. She worked her way quickly down the steps to the ground. Every time the blades clicked she felt better. Finally, the wood became too thick for her shears. She stood back. She could hear her own breath scraping the insides of her ribs and heaving out of her.

As she looked at the pile of branches lying helter-skelter on the ground, a quiet like embers set into her. She climbed back up the steps. Like a sleepwalker, still holding the shears, in both hands, blades pointing forward, she went into the house.

## Sisters

Sister Bernadette was walking in the garden. Green vines gentled the sandstone walls. Plush lawns smoothed the uneven ground. Flowers burst in sprays of white, yellow, pink. The sun was brilliant. She was happy. She was safe. But someone was disturbing her, shaking her awake. She blinked into darkness. She must have overslept. But how could that be? In twenty-four years she had not once been late for morning prayers.

A dark shape floated above her. Then the light came on and a woman's voice said, "Oh, thank heaven." The shape lifted. "I couldn't wake you," the voice kept on. "You were sleeping so soundly."

Sister Bernadette still couldn't see the face. It was all mixed up with her mother's face. She must have been dreaming. She narrowed her eyes.

"It's the phone." The voice was urgent. "For you." She stared a moment longer. "A call, for you," the voice repeated.

As Sister Bernadette got up from her narrow bed and found her robe and slippers, she thought, she's right to be alarmed. For who would phone a monastery at this hour unless it was a disaster?

It was Joseph, long distance. She looked at her watch — ten to four. She knew it must be bad news, and her first thought was of Emily. Why her? she wondered, when it's almost certain to be my mother who, after all, is in her seventies. "Yes," she said, bracing herself.

"No, no," she assured him. "You didn't wake us, wake anybody up."

"That woman..."

"Mother Ignatius. She's on night watch this week. That's one of the things we do, you know, we are committed to, continuous prayer, believing, at the darkest hour..." Why am I going on like this, she thought. He didn't phone in the middle of the night for conversation. "It's all right," she said. "We all get up for prayers soon anyway."

"You know how she's always been able to eat anything." Joseph's voice was strange, a hollow shell where words echoed. What could be so terrible as to shake Joseph? Not ordinary life or death. He had seen too much of that, had inflicted enough of his own. She must listen. What was he saying?

"She's had heartburn, you know, the last few years, kept salts, in the cupboard above the sink, must have forgotten about the lye, must have put it there herself, after dousing out the chicken coup. In the night," came the voice. "Didn't stop to put on the light... must have made a mistake."

He repeated the same details. Why is he talking so much, she thought. He never talks. He never phones long distance. He hates spending money.

Who was he talking about? It could be his wife. Or Emily. Or even one of the children. It could be anyone. But no, she knew. Please don't let it be my mother, she thought. "Who?" she said. "Who?" she repeated, hearing the tightness in her own voice.

"Ma... Ma... I heard something... I found her... I got her to the hospital as fast as I could, but..." A pause. "Can you come?"

Her first response was no. "You know my vows," she said.

"But something like this... I thought they changed the rules."

"Yes, well, some of it is, at least, well, I'll have to ask, find out. When is the funeral? Maybe..."

"Don't know yet," he said. Then, "When you get here."

"Yes, well, I don't know, I'll find out. I'll ask Mother Superior. I'll phone you back, tonight."

"At a time like this," said Joseph, "you'd think..."

This isn't Joseph, she thought. Not this voice. Not this need. She relented. "I'm pretty sure," she said, "but I'd better phone you back anyway."

She knew she had to go. How can you not go to your own mother's funeral? But she couldn't bring herself to say it yet. In the meantime, she must find some words for Joseph. She called up her best sisterly voice, soft yet firm tones. "We will pray," she said. "We will pray for all of you. Bless you and your brave family." She could hear some relief settle into his voice as he said good-bye.

She listened to the hum of the dead receiver. She thought of the complicated system of wires and poles it took to connect her to her brother. They finally got at me, she thought. They reached even into this place. Her mother. It was ironic that her mother should be the one. Her mother who in life made no demands, who understood everything.

But such understanding had been erased from the world. No, not erased—twisted out of the world. Ordinary death was not enough to get rid of such a woman. They had to burn the throat out of her. Sister Bernadette caught herself. She mustn't think, mustn't question... She must think of Joseph. How terrible it must have been. Poor Joseph. But, then, Joseph was the best one... He was the one who could handle it. He was used to... That other time when he found... Joseph, the eldest, the one who took over the farm, the one who took responsibility for their mother and for Emily. Widowed mothers and Emilys, the old and the... people like that had to live somewhere, with somebody, with somebody like Joseph.

She set down the receiver and looked around her. How she loved this place! The hardwood floor gleaming softly in the yellow light, the small desk with its pen in a holder, its notepad placed at just the right angle. How she loved the smells—wax, polish, incense. The voices that soon would come from the chapel would be in perfect harmony.

The killing place, that was how she used to think of it. Sister Bernadette watched the straw tips of her broom reach into crevices between the stones of the walk. She saw a spot cluttered with dirt and dry leaves and attacked with short brusque movements. Concentrate on the job at hand, she told herself. Focus on placing one foot in front of the other. Still, there was virtue in preparation. How to go back to that place without her mother. "Offer it up... sometimes God sends us these things to test us... we must bear crosses without complaint..." she heard her mother's voice. But some crosses seem unbearable. Bernie Neville had thought that, too. Bernie Neville wanted to be asked to the school dance. Bernie Neville knew that something had to be done about Emily.

IHS, Jesus Saviour of Men. Sister Bernadette watched her hands place the wafers into plastic containers, carefully so that the monograms were all exactly on top of each other. In this cross is salvation. Her mother's belief. The only thing that made life bearable out there. But how had that woman held on to such belief? She thought of her father, the way he used to attack the land, the very air itself, his powerful body cutting its way through. Joseph was the same, and the others, Steve, Mike, John. They were all still up there. She was the only one to escape. She could not call her father's release an escape. Her mother, though. Sister Bernadette knew that when she thought of her mother, she must be happy.

The Sisters of the Precious Blood, the straight rows of broad red bands, the lowered black veils. This chapel. Evening meditation, Sister Bernadette's favourite time. Kneeling here, she knew that she was part of something important. This act of beads passing in a circular motion of hands crossed continents, oceans. She was lulled by sounds, whispered prayers, even the inevitable coughing, clearing of throats. She was assured by the pattern of light and shadow falling on the embroidered tapestries, on the stations of the cross. In summer the light angled through stained glass. In winter lamps and candles produced the shadows.

It might not be so bad if it were summer. Why had her mother not died in summer? In summer the country was alive, the days were long. Tomorrow morning she had to get on that bus. She would have to submit to being sucked into a darkness that city people could never understand. Complete blackness, all around her, stretching away for hundreds of miles. There was no place you could run from such blackness, no place, now that her mother was gone.

The circle of light on oilcloth, bright at the centre, spiralling out to where her mother sat, her needle flashing across the heel of a sock or her two needles clicking. Her brothers and Emily, all of them there in the kitchen, fighting, playing, making fudge during sieges of weather. Their mother, stopping the fights, joining in the games, directing the fudge-making.

Their father would open the door and let in a blast of storm. He stamped his feet, hung up his parka, turned with his fierce face, his knotted forehead. Their mother got him something hot to drink. She took food out of the warming oven. Gradually, his face would clear. But in the end her love was no match for his despair. Sister Bernadette wondered if her mother had felt that failure. But then her mother had been mistaken in so many things. She was a woman who let other people use her up and called it love.

She was a woman who would say now, if she could, child, child, don't come if it bothers you so much. I don't mind.

But she must go. She must think of others. Joseph. She had failed him this morning. Why had she not said yes immediately, yes, of course I'll come. Of course. Why could she not have given him that much? But she had not expected *that* Joseph. Dazed, stricken with... What? Grief? It was hard to believe. She saw a face set in grim lines, the eyes cold, always calculating, figuring the exact right moment to tighten a snare, the time of released shot, the distance of small animals. His hands, strong, efficient, slitting open a cow's belly, plucking up kittens by their necks, throwing them into a sack. The kittens were special. Orange kittens. She had followed the orange stray when it came to the back door for scraps, followed it to its litter on the soft ragged seat of a motorless old truck. For several days, she fed the mother. Then Joseph drowned the kittens. The mother looked all over for them, calling and crying, then she disappeared.

Still, she must go. It was expected of her. Mother Superior had said she must leave right away, had phoned the Greyhound depot that very minute. The bus, the one that made the best connections, left early in the morning. A reprieve. One day. What for? Only putting off the inevitable. But kneeling in the warm light, she thought how she had been thankful. The inevitable might not happen. In this extra day she might become ill, break an arm or a leg, a hip. It might be time enough for the world to end.

If it were the old days, she would not have to go. When the Order was truly cloistered. In those days, when she first joined, habits were long, walls firmly in place. She was in Edmonton then. Her family visited more often. They sat, quiet and intimidated, on the other side of the grille. She saw her mother's face, her brothers' faces, through wooden slats. She saw an eye, a section of a cheek, a collar, a buttoned pocket, wisps of her mother's hair.

She traced her beads. She knew this was not the proper way to pray. Going through the motions, her mind revolving on her personal problems rather than her prayers. She made herself concentrate on the feel of the beads, on the words of the prayers, on the vision of her intention, the conversion of sinners. Like myself, she thought. All the poor, tormented creatures of this hateful earth.

She stared out the bus window at the drab November day, at the fields of stubble flecked with snow, at the windbreak trees already drawn into themselves for winter. Mile after mile after mile. It was like a dream of day, of some repeated activity imprinted on the brain. Her face felt as frozen as the land. If she could only sleep, even doze, but her eyes were pinned open.

Two nights, she thought. I only have to get through two nights. Mother Superior told her to stay several days, as long as her family needed her. But she had already decided on excuses for that one. She was a burden to her sister-in-law. There was enough to do without extra house guests. She was in the way.

They were north of Edmonton now. It was getting dark. This was the worst time, when it was coming down. She calculated. Fifteen hours. Fifteen hours to get through. She felt the old panic seize her and tighten around her. There was nothing she could do, any of them could do, to stop the night. She must calm herself. She would manage. After all, she managed before. Bernie Neville was a survivor. That was why she had to do something about Emily.

But then her mother was here. She had always been here. All through her own absence, she was here. Between the rare visits she was here, steady and waiting for her. Sister Bernadette tried to see her mother's face. It must be nearly four years. Joseph brought her south on the bus. The two of them came, in the late fall, after harvest.

"How is Emily?" Sister Bernadette asked.

"Oh, fine," her mother answered.

She searched now as then for a hint, a sign of disapproval, of blame, in her mother's voice. But that was not her mother's way. As far as her mother was concerned, there was no blame. Things had turned out all right. Emily liked it on the farm. She was a big help. Her mother had never admitted that there was anything wrong with Emily. Emily was just different in her own way. Her mother would not even use the word 'slow,' even when Emily was thirteen years old and in grade four.

"That dumb ox," Sister Bernadette heard Bernie Neville say. "She doesn't belong in school."

"She likes school," her mother said. "She's learning lots of things. Maybe she'll learn enough to get a job in town."

"And what about me? The kids think I'm weird, too, because of her."

"Maybe if you're nice to her the others will be."

"How can you be nice to someone like that? She's, she's," Bernie searched for the word. "A retard, that's what she is."

"Maybe she's not so bright in her mind, but she's a person, too."

"She's not a person. You should see the way she eats. Her mouth open.

And she spits out her food. No one will go near her at lunch. And you should see her, sitting with all those kids half her size. It's awful. I can't stand it."

Bernie Neville's solution was to pretend that Emily was not her sister. But, of course, she was, and everybody knew it. One day when the others were making fun of Emily, when they had her backed into a corner of the schoolyard, Bernie watched. Emily didn't understand what was happening, but her eyes were worried. Then she saw her sister. A look of relief washed across her broad face. But Bernie knew in that moment that if she chose Emily, her life at school would be over. It was instinct, she decided later. The way her mouth opened and her voice joined the others. Pain was Emily's first reaction. Pain, then bewilderment.

Bernie was furious. She was close to tears.

"I'm going to quit," she said to her mother that evening. "I'll run away if I have to."

After that Emily was kept home. Every morning her eyes followed Bernie down the lane, waited with her at the stop, climbed up onto the bus with her. In the late afternoon, Emily was waiting by the side of the road. She would take Bernie's lunch pail and swing it along beside her from the road to the house. Every day she asked the same question. "What did you do today?" A year later, Bernie managed to get herself accepted into a convent school in Edmonton.

The bus crossed the Peace, the remembered boundary to the outside, to paradise. Sister Bernadette could not see the river because there was no moon, but she knew it was down there. She knew she was home.

"Things haven't changed much," she said to the boy.

"Don't suppose," he said.

"Your mother wrote about the new ice arena in town. That's different, I guess."

"Yeah, that's pretty nice."

Sister Bernadette watched the headlights of the truck tunnel a path through the darkness. Like cement, she thought. She wanted to ask this boy what her mother had been like these last years. She wanted stories, details. Were you close to your grandmother? she wanted to ask. What did you think about her? But she knew such questions would get her nowhere.

"One thing, there's lots of room," she said. She stretched her legs before her, straight out, in the half-ton pickup. "You get kind of cramped on those buses."

"It's just that Mom 'n Dad took the car," the boy said.

Sister Bernadette looked up at him. He's not a boy, she thought, I must stop thinking of him that way. Eighteen. At the depot, when he suddenly appeared before her, she thought, how can Joseph be so young? Heavyset, solid, the commanding way he stepped into the confusion of suitcases, picked out hers, directed her to his truck. Probably practical, too, she thought, although she didn't know that. She didn't know anything about her nieces and nephews. She had never seen them, let alone talked with them.

"This is just fine," she said, stretching again.

"They thought they'd be back in lots of time," the young man said.

Even the voice. Joseph's. That time Joseph stood in the kitchen doorway, his face completely drained of colour, yet his voice steady.

"What are your plans?" she asked. "Now that you're finished with school."

"Guess I'll stay on the farm."

Already settled, then. Sensible. Mature.

"You like it here, then?" she asked.

"It's okay, I guess."

They turned off the highway onto gravel.

She was dead. Here was the evidence. Sister Bernadette recognized the large rough knuckles laced across the broad bodice. She recognized the dress. How convenient, she thought, that her mother's dress was black. Black rayon, long sleeves, buttons down the front, a thin fabric belt.

She did not recognize the face. The dry cracked lips were red and greasy. The sallow cheeks were pink. The loose skin was filled out. In the words of the community, the undertaker had done a lovely job. She knew now why Joseph had felt better last night. He had been back to normal. She had seen that right away, when he had come into the house, nodded, said hello. They had been at the funeral parlour, he and his wife. They had just viewed the remains, this mask. Joseph had faced a lot in his life. He had faced his father lying in a pool of his own blood. He had cleaned it up, scrubbed it out of the barn boards, made all the arrangements. He could understand his father's death, his father's practical approach to an incurable cancer. But his mother's death was different. It was uncanny, as though an evil force were in control of things.

God's will. She must believe it was God's will. But then it was not fair! It was not fair! If ever a woman deserved to die peacefully in her sleep, it was her mother. A woman who had worked every day of her life from five in the morning until late at night. A woman who had given birth to eight children, buried two. Surely, surely, such a woman deserved... dignity. A perfect ending, she thought, a perfect ending for a stupid, crude existence. The waste of life. Her brothers, a lifetime of rooting things out of the soil like animals. Emily, locked in eternal ignorance. What was the point of it all? Of anything? Her head felt wound around and around with the layers of her thoughts. The words of the mass were muffled. "Eternal rest give to them, O Lord, and let perpetual light shine upon them."

The congregation passed through the doorway of the church and stepped out into a cold wind. Sister Bernadette was walking beside Joseph. At the bottom of the steps he stopped her. She saw his hand on her white immaculate sleeve. He had scrubbed his hands with a brush, but nothing could remove the stains of earth, of grease and oil. Nothing could remove the lines and scars. She looked at his face. In the afternoon light, she saw the effects of weather and age. She saw the face of a man who had been forced to grow up too quickly, who knew better than to get excited, who knew that he had to have a certain kind of control or he could not live. Last night they had sat and talked, drinking coffee at the kitchen table. "It was seeing her like that..." he had said, "...it was the way... you know, it shook me... there was something about seeing her like that..."

Last night she had thought how closed his face was, the jaw set, the mouth in a straight line. It had recalled to her another time. As children once they had come upon a dead animal, a heifer, with certain soft parts missing. There had been a rash of such deaths in the country. Some people spoke of evil cults, rites by the full moon, offerings and sacrifice. Their father had said no. That was all superstitious nonsense. It was a virus going around. Certain birds and animals, scavengers, took advantage of the situation and went for those parts. As children, they had listened to their father. They wanted to believe there was a reason for things. They had to believe.

It wasn't grief, she thought, as people gathered around them, as hands reached to extend sympathy, as groups of people floated them away from each other. The reason his voice had been so strange on the phone. What she had heard over the phone was the shock of seeing something he did not want to believe. There are things we can not talk about. Things connected with this place. Things that are too horrible.

"Maybe," said Joseph before they were cut off, "if Emily isn't home when we get there, you could go find her. The wife'll be pretty busy with the lunch."

"Will she know me?" she asked.

"She knows you're her sister. That's all she needs to know."

Sister Bernadette walked through the field. Bare bushes made her think of barbed wire bales in war prison pictures. Tree skeletons against the bleak sky made her think of the last judgement. Dead grass scratching her ankles might have been burnt by final destruction. This place is cursed, she thought, cursed and abandoned. She looked up. The old house crouched low to the earth.

It had never been painted. They could never afford paint. Her parents had built it themselves. There was nothing here then. Stories. She knew the stories. Everyone had stories. Her mother's stories – alone in winter with the children and hardly any food. Her father had gone off to find work. Otherwise, they would have starved. They couldn't make enough with the prices what they were then. The closest doctor was twenty-five miles, and they did not have a horse. They weren't the only ones in this situation. Children died. Often no one knew why. People birthed and buried their own children. There were fevers, infections. There were deformities, terrible scars, accidents.

Emily, she thought. Is she hiding from me? Last evening when she arrived Emily was already in bed, and this morning she had already disappeared. When they were ready to leave for the church, no one could find her. "Does she do this often?" she had asked Joseph. "Disappear, I mean."

"Not disappear so much. Just forgets. You know she always was kind of vague like that. Usually she goes and sits out by the old house. That's probably where she'll be when we get back."

Near one of the walls Sister Bernadette saw a dark shape. It looked like a mole burrowing into the earth. "So this is where you are," she said, coming up behind it. "This is where you've been hiding." She knew her voice sounded forced, too cheerful.

Emily turned her face up so quickly Sister Bernadette could not escape it. It was the face of a middle-aged woman. It was her mother's face. Even the lines were in the same places, deep across the forehead, vertical cuts near the mouth. She saw her mother's wispy greying hair. She saw her mother's eyes. They were happy to see her.

She doesn't know who I am, thought Sister Bernadette. She doesn't remember.

"Bernie," Emily said. Even her voice was like their mother's. Even her smile. She stood up slowly. She put her arms around her sister.

Sister Bernadette felt herself held by strong arms against a strong body. "You have to forgive yourself," her mother had said. She had forgotten that. But now she remembered how they were standing on the sidewalk in front of Ken's Service Station, the bus stop then. Her mother held her just like this. That must have been the last time. After that there was always the cloister window between them. "Otherwise you're no good to anybody," her mother had said close to her ear. "If you want to do something for Emily, that's what you can do."

At the time she had thought the words strange. She did not know what "forgive" meant. Why would she want to do something for Emily? In the excitement of the trip, she had quickly forgotten the incident. How did she know? wondered Sister Bernadette, her face pressed against her sister's. How had her mother known more about her than she herself had known? And Emily, too, she thought. She knows all about me, and she still loves me. If she loves me, maybe I can love myself.

When the two women walked back across the field the lights were on. Lights fanned from windows of the new bungalow, making wide bands of yellow on the frozen ground. Lights came from the barn and the machine shed. A high voltage light on a tall pole lit up the whole farmyard. In the house, through the windows, Sister Bernadette could see all the people who had come to say good-bye to her mother. They were talking and laughing. They were having a good time. This is the way it should be, she thought.

## Daniel

Daniel straightens his shoulders. Inside the pockets of his ski jacket he flexes his fingers. They are frozen into fists. His stomach growls with hunger. That and his hiking boots creaking against old snow are the only sounds. He looks up. His eyes are clear green, his eyebrows and hair nearly black, a contrast to the white all around him.

He sees the lane before him and to the side clotheslines hung with rigid shapes — shirts, nightgowns, a pair of men's long underwear, spread-eagled. Monday. For some people Monday will always be washday. And in this neighbourhood the women do not trust dryers. Both his mother and his aunt said that dryers yellowed things and that things smelled nicer if they were hung outside. This is the right place for them, he thinks, the right place for these people. Here they can do no harm. Here, he decides, they can't hurt me. All I have to do is stay away, visit occasionally and judiciously. Judiciously. He says it out loud, rolling the acquired word from his tongue. His lips are numb.

Sunday and their voices, worry for the old man:
His mother,"Why don't you go and see for yourself?" And at the door when he was leaving, "Just don't expect too much."
His father, "At times, y'know, he thinks he can go back to the farm. No need to tell him any different. Just upset him."
"But he's the one who sold it!" He thought he had missed something.

And his mother's, "Ah, well, he just gets addled sometimes, like the rest of us. And who has the better right? He'll be seventy-eight next month."

And his, "He's all right, isn't he?"

And his father's, "Oh yes. Not like some people with strokes who go all paralyzed."

"Oh, at first, a bit, the one side," put in his mother. "But he came back real good."

"Constitution of a horse," his father.

His sister, "He's awfully thin."

His mother, "Well, and was he ever fat?"

His father, "No, not fat. Lean as a whip, and strong. They say that's what saved him, his good health, y'know."

"You'll see for yourself next week then." His mother placed her hand on his sleeve. He was out the door.

She meant last week. Here it was, another Monday. This morning he told himself he had to. He couldn't face another family dinner without going to see his grandfather. He knew he shouldn't have left it this long.

His ears ache. He cups his hands over them. The blood drains, exposing his fingers to frostbite. He puts his hands back in his pockets and thinks how he should have worn a toque and gloves. His father used to read them the story about the man building the fire. At the end of the story, when the man is freezing to death, he seems to be outside himself, looking for himself, finding himself frozen in the snow. His father used to remind them of this story any time they were, in his words, running around like chickens with their heads cut off.

Follow the rules. He should have eaten today. It must be nearly five o'clock. His fridge this morning—one case of beer bottles, empty except for one; two smeary cups full of bacon grease. His mother always saves bacon grease. Throwing it out seems at least a venial sin.

Lisa, "What are you saving *that* for? All that cholesterol?"

She stood, tolerant and amused, leaning against the kitchen counter, her robe loose and open at the top. Other Sundays. They slept late and he whomped up enormous breakfasts which she ate, to please him more than anything.

"That's good stuff," he told her. "Next week we'll fry up some potatoes."

But they never did. In the two years they were together, they never bought potatoes. Potatoes were too complicated for their lifestyle. They ate a lot of minute rice.

He used to like the cold. When he was a child, cold was his friend. He watched out the window for it, so he could skate, toboggan, ski, so he and his brothers and sisters and cousins could build snow forts and throw snowballs. Wet snow is best for that. Today's snow is dry. Its moisture has evaporated. It sits, a crusty froth, on roofs, fences. He has an impulse to take a stick, run it along the edge of the fence. But he knows that would be immature.

"Live a little," Lisa said when he was being what she considered too serious. "You're such a square," she teased. When had her voice taken on an edge?

"Laughing causes less lines than worrying," his aunt said. "Or at least sets them in the right direction."

Lisa. His aunt on the phone. Lisa, the last time he saw her. His aunt on the phone this morning. Lisa. What went wrong? But he had sworn off thoughts of Lisa. It was necessary. He had to get through papers, exams. That first week, before he got a grip on himself, it was like his mind was caught on a revolving wheel and couldn't get off.

His aunt on the phone. "Don't be too early. He always has his nap right away after lunch. If he misses it there's no living with him. I won't tell him you're coming either, until after his nap. He'll get himself too excited to sleep."

Who were we talking about? Daniel wonders. He can't imagine anyone speaking that way about his grandfather. He sees a face, a strong face, a determined jaw, the hair a wild white bush. He sees himself sitting across from that face, a crib board on the cleared dining table between them.

"The spitting image," the voices say.

"A chip off the old block."

"That acorn didn't fall far from the tree."

Birds fly, fall, around him. A flock of starlings. Like blown bits of carbon paper they rise and drift down to rest in back gardens, on snow-covered clods of broken earth and compost heaps silent as burial mounds. Some light on telephone poles, tall black crosses against the white February sky.

His hunger rolls in the hollow inside him. "He comes home now and then," his mother said, "to get a decent meal." She thought she was joking. Since Lisa left there is never any food at his place. He is starving all the time now.

Soup. Soup in the cafeteria. That day they met by accident. Two weeks, three days, and how many hours ago? "You wanted to know everything," he accused.

"I meant harmless things. Like what you did as a kid and all."

She tipped the bowl away from herself and levelled off a spoonful.

Her house. Her parents' house. At table. They ate on a cloth, even on weekdays. The food, on plates brought from the kitchen. A meat, a vegetable, a baked potato wrapped in tin foil. Nothing touched. That first time when he was being inspected. He did not know how to eat. No one had taught him. Dessert. He was spouting off to Lisa's father, his opinions, politics. He wolfed down some pink concoction before he noticed that the others had not started on theirs. Except Lisa. She was loyally picking away at the edges of hers. But then he noticed her spoon, a different spoon, larger than the one he had used, and the one meant for him, along the top of his table setting, where it continued to lie, heavy and accusing, throughout the remainder of the meal.

He winces with pain. But he never let that sort of thing happen again. Now he waits and watches.

"Keep your fork, there's pie!" His mother, his various aunts.

The table, long, two tables put together, card tables for the children. The food—great vats and bowls and platters of it. His plate, layers, like archaeological digs. The platters passed clockwise, potatoes, turkey, stuffing, cabbage rolls, cranberry sauce, carrots, peas, two salads, buns. A mountain. Gravy on everything, please.

The voices of men:

"Ah, I tell y' we had happy chickens then. Not like now. Have y' seen the way they gottem all cooped up in them little boxes? We let them have the run of the place. And we had the better eggs for it too. Am I right?"

"Right as rain."

"It's the government getting in where they don't belong. You take the price of meat now in the store and what the farmer gets. No, there's something wrong somewhere when it comes to that."

"Still, then, when it comes to a place where they should interfere, they don't. I'm thinking of corporate profit. Oh yes, the sky's the limit there, but when it comes to the little man, the man on the street..."

When did he graduate to that table? From the card table? In his turn.

"Now is that enough for y' Dan? A great lunking thing like you needs a full plate."

"We're to have a barrister and solicitor in the family then. It's proud we are of you. You'll be the first in the family to take a university degree."

"Ah, well, our generation didn't have the opportunities."

"And don't be forgettin' the brains."

"Oh yes, the brains are important too, no doubt of it."

"I might be wrong about this, but the way it seems t'me, most people's got pretty well the same amount of brain. It's what you do with em that counts."

"Like Steve now. You couldn't find a brighter boy. And one thing about Steve, he'd give you the shirt off his back. But he never was much for drive."

"To each his own."

"Danny here has the drive. I'll give him that."

One day he surprised himself with his own voice. "My name is Daniel."

His uncle, "And a good name it is too. A young man who kept his faith even in the fiery furnace."

"That was Shadrach, Meshach and Abednego."

"Quite right, quite right. They're in the same book. That is the book of Daniel. It was the lion's den then, for Daniel, I've got it now."

His grandfather sat directly across the table from him. He felt the old man's studying look. He knew he had been rude to his uncle. His uncle had bought him his first ice cream cone. He had taken them all to the Exhibition, all the children who were in existence then. Daniel's mother was in the hospital having her latest. He would never forget that first lick across the cream, smooth and icy on his tongue. The world was certainly a place of marvels and delights.

He could not raise his head to meet his grandfather's eyes.

Was that the last time I saw him? wonders Daniel. And when was that? Two Christmases ago? Last Christmas with Lisa and her family. The tree was a perfect shape, all in blue, blue lights, blue globes, blue tinsel. The gifts beneath the tree might have been professionally wrapped.

No, not Christmas. It was a christening. His sister's child. His niece, his parents' granddaughter, his grandfather's great-granddaughter.

It is a long lane. There's a bend in the middle. Where normally a street would cut through. How they used to travel this lane! His brothers and sisters, his cousins. Always running back and forth between the two houses.

This was their territory. Their games – hide and seek, crouched behind ripe pumpkins, rain barrels, cold frames stacked for storage. The tension between being caught and making home free. Street hockey in winter twilight, slap of stick and puck. And later, engine parts scattered behind garages. The satisfying rev when some reconstructed wonder actually worked. Too quiet now. Where is the sound of traffic? Where is everyone? People calling to each other across fences? But he's thinking of summers. This cold is heavy. It muffles sound.

Why does he have the feeling that he is being watched? By those old windows. By those houses tall and narrow as nuns. They are listening, too. To the uncanny silence. He shivers. He knows it is not possible for a person to freeze to death in the middle of a city, but he has forgotten how cold a person can get walking only a few blocks in this weather.

A mood like still black water. A reservoir on the farm, in the cellar, a bottomless pool. Nightmares of falling in. He senses danger. It is dangerous to let your thoughts control you.

His mother would say the trouble is food. "I don't like to see you so thin," she said. Only minutes ago. When he left his car and said he'd walk.

"I need the exercise," he said.

The truth is, he feels a need to prepare himself.

*Hungry, hungry, I am hungry; table, table, here I come.* The old children's song bounces through his head.

Maybe he has let himself go too far. Maybe his body is starting to devour itself. Maybe he cannot reverse the process.

His aunt on the phone, "It's a long time since you've tasted my Yorkshire pudding." Trust her to remember! His favourite! It used to be nothing for him to polish off half a pan of it. The bottom, baked and crisped in beef fat, and soaking into it, the gravy, brown and smooth. The beef itself, the rind roasted to caramel brown. He can smell it. He can see the way it will look steaming on his plate. He can taste it.

He places one foot before the other. His boots have red laces. Red trails of blood. Blood in the snow.

"Blood is thicker than water." His mother.

There is no answer to such infuriating clichés. Before each visit he takes a vow of silence. That is the mature thing to do. They haven't a clue. No wonder he never let them and Lisa meet. It would have been a disaster.

It was a disaster anyway.

A perfect moment. A dreaming moment. They spoke of marriage. Even children.

Lisa, "I like the name Crystal."

"What kind of name is that?" He meant his voice to be light. Why did it emerge inflexible?

"A nice name. Clarity. A bell."

"Any kid of mine will have a decent name."

"What's a decent name?" The tone of her voice should have warned him.

"Ann, James, Stephen."

"Saint names. I'm onto you." Lightening her voice, trying to keep things on a safe level.

"Saint names or not, they're not just fads because of some movie star or hockey star."

It ended, as it so often did, with Lisa shouting, jumping off the bed, slamming into the bathroom.

He never shouted in return. He thought the best thing was to turn away. This drove her into further frenzies. But he was pleased at his control.

Sunday. He snatched the can opener from his mother's hand, applied it expertly to the can, slammed both it and the can back down on the counter, flung himself back onto the bench.

Pure loss of control, he thinks. But that's the effect they have on him. How can he help it? His mother, "Ah, well, your old mom isn't as young as she used to be." Puzzling over what she called "this new-fangled gadget." They let themselves become old, he decides. They take satisfaction in defeat, in the repetition of communal destiny.

But his mother didn't see. She picked up a fork and jabbed at something in a pot. "Sometimes I wonder," she said in a voice of gentle anxiety, "if all that studying is good for you."

His temper. A slip. He must admit. As a child he had a terrible temper. An Irish temper, the family called it, something like pride in their voices. Once when he was fighting with his brother, he smashed his fist through a window, aiming for his brother's face on the other side. His fist was covered with blood. But he had learned to control that temper. Usually.

"Past history," he told Lisa. "It can't hurt you, unless you let it."

His name, too. There is no reason why he has to keep his name. That's what he wanted to tell them, his mother, Lisa.

She wanted to get married right away. He wanted to wait. "Someday," he said, "I'll be able to give you everything." He told her of his plan to change his name.

"Why would you want to do something like that?" she screeched. "O'Reilly is a perfect name!"

"Nothing drastic," he assured. "Only the O. Only dropping the O."

"But why?"

He tried to explain. O'Reilly is a ridiculous name. "It makes you think of barroom brawls," he said, "shady politics, Paddy's pig, all those ethnic jokes. It's not the right sort of name for a professional man. Lyons," he said. "Something like Lyons would be perfect. Even Smith." But he had no intention of being that extreme. All he wanted was to subdue the name a little, make it more suitable for a dignified lawyer.

His mother was even worse. She stood at the kitchen counter. He sat on the bench where he always sat when he wanted to talk with her. His long legs stuck out partway into the room, the way they always did, so that she had to move around them. He shifted in apology and she said no, no, she liked them there. She liked knowing he was there.

He was trying to think of a way to introduce the subject. It was going to be a tough proposal. That was why he decided to tackle her first, before his father. "O'Reilly," he said. "What kind of name is that anyway?"

"Well," she said, distracted by the new can opener in her hand, "the O'Reillys know who they are."

That was as far as he got. His temper intervened.

She always did that. Blocked communication with an undebatable state-ment. His first years at university. He had been introduced to Voltaire in a French course. He tried to tell her about the new ideas he was ex-periencing. "Fancy talk," she said, "for being too lazy to get up and go to Mass Sunday morning."

It's their own fault I left them, he decides. But their intention is to reclaim him from exile. He knows it. This spring. "You'll soon be finished," his sister said, meaning finished with the books. They think he has simply been away for awhile. They do not realize that he is into another life from

which he can never return. He will not let himself return. He must hold
out against returning. The thought of returning fills him with dread. Returning to mediocrity, lack of intellectual stimulation, death. He will not let
himself be caught. He will resist guilt. It's a matter of avoiding traps. His
father's, "It'd do his heart good." His mother's, "He asks about you all the
time."

He wasn't here for the stroke. It wasn't his fault. He was out of town
most of last summer working for the highways department on a road construction crew. He was in the city on weekends, most weekends, but then
there was Lisa. He found out about his grandfather when it was all over.
He phoned his mother, a routine call. His grandfather was already out
of the hospital, back with his aunt and uncle who had more room.

Nothing can kill a tough old bird like that, he told himself.

"Dan O'Reilly," he whispers the name to the cold air. For a moment
it takes shape. Then it drifts away. Grandfather. That is the word in Lisa's
family, but it does not fit the man who waits for him at the end of this
lane. *Grampa.* That's the word. The childhood name. *Grampa* is someone
who drinks straight whiskey from a water tumbler, someone who gives
you a dollar for a can of pop and never asks for the change, someone
who stands at a black iron farmhouse stove at five in the morning flipping
pancakes onto your plate as fast as you can gobble them down. Someone
who shouts, "You can't wrestle life on an empty stomach!"

Daniel squirms inside and frowns outside. The past is irrelevant. It
doesn't exist any more than that farm hacked up and parcelled out by
developers. That's what he told Lisa.

"Start from the beginning," she said that first night. "And tell me
everything."

And he did. Not that first night, but over the two years. Was that what
went wrong? Did he tell her too much?

His grandfather and the farm, those long summers of batching, the two
of them. They ate a lot of stew. It took only one pot. "All ends up in the
same place anyway!" his grandfather would shout. Cleaning up the place
the evening before his parents were due to arrive to take him home for
school. His grandfather turfing the piled-up potato peelings into a bucket
for him to take out to the pigs. "Yer ma'll never let you come again if she
sees this!"

"I should have known," Daniel said to her.

"But how could you?"

"Why else would he hang on, already past seventy."

He told her about telling his grandfather that he had registered for the fall term at university. "He just seemed to cave in," he confessed, "just for a minute. But then his voice came strong. 'Oh, y' vex me so,' he said. 'Now get away with you, go on home now, all of you.' I went outside," said Daniel. "I could hear my Dad, 'the boy just don't want to be a farmer.' I swear that was the first I thought of it."

"It wasn't your fault," Lisa said. "And how about your brothers or all those cousins? It's not as though you're the only one."

"I was his favourite," Daniel explained. "And the oldest boy. I was given the name. Anyway, no one else wanted it either."

"It is a terrible thing," said Lisa. "When you stop and think about it."

"What could I do?" said Daniel. "It wasn't my fault."

"No, of course not," she said.

His father, sitting at the head, looking at him across a table heavy with food. His father's voice, "What is it you want, son?"

When they were children, his father took them to the playground, all six of them, in the warm evenings of summer, after supper while their mother tidied up the kitchen, or on Sunday afternoon while she was busy preparing the meal. There he settled himself on a bench and watched them crawl through the maze built into an oversized tree trunk. He watched them pump themselves on the swings, high, higher. Sometimes he pushed the smallest ones who had not yet learned to pump, or he filled in as a partner on the teeter-totter, his long legs reaching to the ground. When they scratched or scraped themselves, his father looked at the injury for a long time, then promised mercurochrome and band-aids when they got home. On the way home, they often stopped at his uncle's, and his aunt hauled popsicles or ice cream out of the fridge. The adults sat on the porch and watched the children running and shouting in the yard, his aunt calling out for them to be careful of her garden.

The garden is empty now except for a chicken wire skeleton growing out of the snow. The house comes out of the dusk like a ghost ship, silent and floating in its own shadows. Once, all the windows were lighted. Now there is only one light, in the downstairs kitchen.

Daniel stands outside the fence. Shadows are only shadows, he thinks. They can't hurt you. If you turn on the light they vanish.

He opens and closes the gate. He starts up the walk. The smell of roast beef is now a reality.

The food on the farm. The food of life, his grandfather called it. Cream so thick you had to spoon it out of the pitcher onto your porridge, fresh butter and buttermilk, delicately salty, drinking warm milk from the cow's teat, Grampa tilting himself back on the stool, white jetting against the tin of the pail. "Hey Dan, c'mere," and a squirt of milk into his mouth. Sometimes it didn't make a direct hit and he would be laughing with the milk dribbling down the side of his face. Kneeling in the hay, the way the hay smelled, the smells of manure and fresh milk. When he was older he did the milking. He would lean forward and rest the side of his face against the soft full belly of the cow.

In the kitchen his aunt's shape moves between fridge and stove. Upstairs the windows are black. He sees something. A movement. He narrows his eyes. He can't tell whether it is something inside the glass or a reflection from outside. Then the window lights up from behind, suddenly. There is a face, a small twisted face pressed up against the glass. He senses that it has been there a long time. Waiting. Its bones are caved in. The eyes are sunk back into the bone. The creature that owns the face claps its hands.

They were worried about me, thinks Daniel. The anxiety in their voices was for me. Not the old man. Me. The old man, like idiots and small children, is in a state of perpetual grace.

The smell of the beef fat turns his stomach. Food is another trap. He cannot go into that house. He cannot eat. He will never be able to eat again. He turns, walks quickly, almost runs, back through the gate and into the lane. Behind him someone laughs.

In the dim light, the lane appears flat. He forgets the ruts. He stumbles and falls. For a moment, he is stunned. Then he becomes aware of himself, his position, his ridiculous position, on hands and knees. He gets up, brushes his jeans with his hands, notices his hands are bleeding, that they are stuck with bits of gravel. He thinks maybe he should go back to his aunt's. But then he knows with certainty that no one can help him, there is no one stronger than himself. He is alone. For a moment he is afraid.

He doesn't know how he will live this way. Then he decides that he doesn't want anyone's help. He will use his loneliness as a weapon against the world. It will make him strong. A rush of quiet fills him. He feels peaceful, almost drowsy, now that he has reached this conclusion.

## Of Love and Bad Guys

This is the story of my father and my father's story and the story of me. I didn't know that at first, I mean the part about it being about me. In fact, I had one hell of a time with this story. At first, I couldn't squeeze it out at all. I could not birth this fossilized fetus. Then it came in the form of a stillbirth, ineffectual and pitiful. It came the wrong way in several drafts, feet first, sideways, any which way but right, normal. Years passed before I understood why. I was writing about my father's failure and I should have been writing about my own.

Poe started me on the realization of my problem. As in Edgar Allan. His story begins "There are some secrets which do not permit themselves to be told." Knowing Poe, you might guess these are the secrets not of others but of ourselves. Those deep dark squiggly secrets, those nightmare worms that coil in our subconscious, that eat the core of our brains in sleep, and that we can't place when we awake. They are why we like horror stories, distant stories in which we can take vicarious pleasure. We are greedy for blood and gore and perversion, as long as it happens to someone else.

Charles Olson via Eli Mandel helped me into final realization. "I take SPACE to be the central fact to man born in America," Mandel quotes Olson in the former's "Strange Loops." "Some men ride on such space, others have to fasten themselves like a stake to survive. As I see it Poe dug in and Melville mounted. They are the alternatives."

I always thought my father was Melville and he turned out to be Poe.

My father smelled of prairie wind and grain and man's sweat. His voice was deep and resonant. It could explode with authority or be seductive as velvet. His face was craggy as a strong cliff. His word was law, at home, in town, in the beer parlour, in council. Even at seventy-nine, he was a large imposing figure. He lived in the city with us then. My mother had died six years earlier. Dad could have lived on his own, stayed on the farm with the land rented out. He could have gotten himself a place in town. But there was one thing Dad needed, and that was to talk. Well, maybe two things; he also needed a receptive ear.

Sometimes we come to knowledge slowly over a period of years. Sometimes it strikes in a moment, like a boa from the branch of a sheltering tree. That's what happened to me. It dropped on an innocent evening in August, an evening like all the others.

"Alex Jones." Dad's voice coiled out of the warm dusk. "When I went in," he was saying, "I usually stayed with Alex. He lived right next to the swamp so it was handy for cutting."

I recognized the name. Alex was the one who had a wife called Mavis. The first time Dad saw her she was sitting in a roadside ditch near town peddling saskatoon berries.

"Like a mirage," as Dad used to tell it. "An afternoon in July, hot enough to fry spit in mid-air."

They were all out on the patio. It was a Sunday evening. Dave had barbecued a standing rib for dinner, what I grew up calling supper, what Dad always called supper. I was in the kitchen, putting the last load of dishes for the day into the dishwasher. The kitchen was dim, but I didn't want to turn on the light.

"A long way," Dad was saying. "Twenty miles. Seems like a hen's trot now. Paved road and a warm car. But then, walking it, behind the horses, thirty below, into the swamps beyond the river, into the bush country, into cold, into nothing but space... a man could freeze to death, a man could disappear without a trace."

Dad's stories did at times verge on rhetoric, it's true, but that didn't diminish them. Rhetoric has fallen into disrepute as an exaggerated use of language, an attempt to sway or persuade. It is now connected with dishonesty. We forget that it used to be a legitimate art. And, after all, what is a man's speech if not the attempt to influence the thought and conduct of his audience.

I scraped meat scraps into the plastic garbage bag beneath the sink and pushed salad trimmings into the garburator, my body on automatic. My ears were not tuned to Dad's actual voice but to his voice inside me. His stories were all recorded in me, and I could play any one I wished. At that moment, I was listening to the Mavis story. I had heard it so many times, I could recall the words verbatim and Dad's voice as he told it. "Well, I stopped and I could see how them berries were going all dried out in the heat. So I bought them all from her, the works, for a dollar, which was twice what she was asking. But what does a bachelor want with three quarts of saskatoons? Oh, I could whip up a mean batch of bannock, but I wasn't much for pie making. So I says to her, well, she'd better take them on home and bake up some pies and invite me for dinner. I was just joking, of course. I had no intention of going twenty miles for pie. But then she smiles up at me and says okay, so then what could I do? So the next day finds me hitching up my wagon and going all that way over them dusty rutted roads just for a slice of pie."

"But most of them poor devils never could get their horses shod," Dad's real voice from the patio was saying. "Couldn't afford nails let alone shoes. And a horse can't do much pulling except on level ground, just shod on front. But to snake a load of fifty posts up that Wimot Hill, in winter. . ."

The voice I heard was his Mavis voice, softer, slower. It was punctuated with pauses, and I was jealous of what went on in those silences.

"What did she look like?" I demanded once.

"Oh, like all the others."

"What's that like?"

"They had a hard life. Aged young."

"So she wasn't pretty?"

"Didn't say that."

"Well, was she?"

"Not pretty, no, you wouldn't call her pretty. Too thin. Made her mouth and eyes look too big."

"What then?" Silence. "Dad..."

"Well, if you must know, there was something about her, tragic like, something haunting. She had a couple of kids, close in age, about eight or nine, a boy and a girl. But she'd buried a couple more. On some dried-out farm back in Saskatchewan."

Two things intrigued me about the Mavis stories. One was the way Dad's voice changed when he told them. The other was that they didn't start until after mother died.

"What's snaking Grampa?" Brian's voice, high and clear, brought me back to the present.

"Oh honestly. Grampa's told you a dozen times." That was Helen, her voice so full of boredom you could slice it. She was twelve, then, and had no patience with any story that wasn't about love. Plus, her definition of love excluded all but the young and good-looking. Old flesh coming together for purposes of sex, although her mind would not have taken it that far but only up to the idea of romance, she would have thought unspeakably repulsive.

As for six-year-old Brian—"Hey Grampa," he would say, climbing up on Dad's lap. "Tell me a story."

"What kind of story?" Dad would ask, knowing full well.

"A story about bad guys," Brian would say with confidence.

Sometimes I took Dad to task about his bad guy stories. The one about the two brothers who pushed the government man into the well was to me particularly spine-chilling. It seemed the man was investigating a report of poaching. The brothers hinted that if there was such a thing as a carcass around in this heat it'd have to be hanging down the well. Then when he bent in to have a look, they toppled him over the edge. The well was dry but deep, and the story went that the man's voice came out of it for days, hollow and echoing, becoming more and more feeble.

"He'll have nightmares," I accused.

"Naw," said Dad. "As long as they're stories that can't happen to him."

So you see, Dad warned me about that distance, the one that must be solidly in place between the story and the teller. That's how you make the story safe for others. That's how you make the story safe for yourself.

I flipped the dishwasher lock and turned the dial to regular wash. "Just take a chain," Dad was saying. "Hitch that to the end of the tongue of the sleigh, ahead of the other team, and then instead of two horses that can't make the hill you got four that can. Then I'd go back down, y'see, and get my own load."

"That must have been hard on the horses." Dave's voice dispensed interest and I breathed a sigh of relief. He was not going to disappear into the bathroom with his latest issue of *Maclean's*. He was going to be professional. When Dave was, or is, for that matter, the impartial observer, which is to say when he puts his mind to it, he can get blood out of a stone. He's not insincere. It's his job. A doctor has to encourage people to tell him everything. He pretends interest and they spill their guts. It's not exactly immoral. He needs their guts for his study and diagnosis.

Not that Dave didn't like Dad. When they first met he found him interesting and entertaining. He told me this. "That was when I'd heard his stories once," Dave said. "Or maybe twice."

When Dad first came to live with us, Dave was determinedly pleasant. He's that kind of man. He was brought up to be polite in social situations and to respect his elders. Then, as the weeks passed, the expression on his face when he saw Dad coming became more and more remote. But that's Dave for you. He doesn't complain or argue. He simply makes statements. Detaching himself is one of them. This makes him rather stern, but I like him this way. He inspires confidence, which is necessary for a doctor. The one time I saw him cry, at his father's funeral, I didn't like the feeling it gave me.

But to continue with my story, which is to say my father's story, through the hum of the dishwasher motor, came Dad's pioneer community philosophy. "Well, you just did it. I had a good team, shod all the way around. And you couldn't leave the poor devils sitting there so you just snaked em up the hill and it meant your horses had to have more rest on the way home."

Like most older people, Dad was always comparing the past and the present. "People don't need each other anymore," he would say, watching Brian and Helen leaving for school in the morning, going in different directions. "Those Jones kids," he would tell me, "the two of em would pile on one old nag and off they'd go. Mavis'd say, 'Be sure and take care of each other now.' " He would turn from the window, back into the kitchen. We would have a cup of coffee together (oh, how I long for the safeness of those moments, before I knew the truth). "Now we got central heating and private rooms," he would say. "In them days you counted on your brothers and sisters in bed at night to keep you from freezing. There's something about sharing the same bed, you can't help but talk."

I wouldn't know about brothers and sisters, since I'm an only child. I do know I don't like confessions. Even during those teenage years when most girls blab half the night, I always found in the end it destroyed the relationship.

"But then what happened if you got caught?" Brian's voice, sharp as a sandpiper's, cleared my head again.

"Well, then the government man made you scatter your load of logs, because you were supposed to pay stumpage on what you cut. It was just like poaching, y'see, only poaching logs instead of game. But no one had any money to pay anything, y'see. But those government men, they didn't like going out there, into that no man's land across the ice. So what they'd do, they'd wait until a man was near town with his load and then catch him. Left some bitter feelings all right. It was no easy job, cutting them logs, wading through snow up to your crotch, pulling them out and loading up your sleigh, then to lose it all."

"But that didn't stop you." Brian's voice was full of admiration.

"Well, what were you gonna do? You had to make a buck any way you could. You couldn't be like a coyote, sit on your backside and howl."

"You were a bad guy too!"

"Well, in the strict sense of the word. I stole as much as anybody. But some laws don't make sense. And when a man's starving, or when he's full of hate, or love, he doesn't think about laws, at least man-made ones."

Dad spoke in a voice which defeated discussion. By making his statements he confirmed himself. That's what I used to tell Dave. "He has to tell stories," I said. "That's why he's still going strong."

I might have added, "and he needs an audience." But Dave knew that. If nothing else, it was evident in the way Dad missed Mother something terrible when she died. The funny thing, though, they had this lifelong running disagreement. "When it comes to marriage," Dad would say, "we get what we deserve." He was joking of course. Still, it bothered me, his ironic sarcasm, her mild disgust. Not that I wanted romance. Like most children I would have found that embarrassing.

Sometimes I wondered why Dad and Mother got married. Oh, I knew the story. Mother was a mail order bride. She answered an advertisement that Dad put in an English newspaper. They met at the old CP station in Calgary on a two-hour stopover. They said hello, had a cup of tea, and got married. Then Mother got back on the train and went to Banff for a holiday. Dad got back into his wagon and went back to his farm. It seems the price on the train ticket was the Special, the same for Banff as for Calgary. Even then, I guess, they were promoting tourism. Since Mother had heard a lot about the Banff Mountain Resort and always wanted to go there, she figured now, or then, was as good a time as any. She was going in that direction anyway. She always said how she was glad she had gone, too, because she didn't have another chance for fifteen years, until after the war and times were better. Anyway, a week later the Addisons, neighbours of Dad, who owned an old Dodge coupe and went up to the hotsprings for her rheumatism, delivered Mother to Dad's doorstep.

"And she never did fully recover, did you, Mother?" Dad used to say, turning on her a quizzical look. He meant from that seven-hour trip on a baking summer day, over a dirt road, lodged between Joyce and Henry Addison. The only possible position for her legs was to straddle them around the floor gearshift. "Yes, boys," Dad would finish, "it set the mood for the rest of our married life."

"And no wonder," Mother would say, turning to the audience. "What he didn't tell you is how in those days when a tire was worn thin or had holes in it, how they took another tire and cut it down and rammed it inside. All I have to do is think of that day and I get motion sickness all over again." Somehow, when she said this, the story was no longer funny. Mother always had this effect on a story. I think it was the tone of her voice, a worried searching tone. All of a sudden the story became too real. You sensed things like pain, suffering, disillusionment.

Dad made a lot of cracks about Mother's English sensibility. His farm had been a favourite stopping place for his bachelor cronies. After he got married they dropped in once, maybe twice, but Mother's housekeeping and refined ways discouraged them. But then why did he send for Mother? If he didn't want a wife?

Back in the innocence of that August evening, before it turned on me, I waited by the patio door for the appropriate moment to take Brian off to bed. For the break between stories. "Olaf Larson," Dad said and I timed him at five minutes.

Olaf is the one who would wait for Dad at the bottom of the hill. He would have started a fire and be brewing tea in a lard pail. He is the one who kept his ear to the grapevine. When he heard that Dad was hauling logs to town, he'd beat him out the next morning and be waiting. He is the man Alex refused to snake up the hill once. As Dad tells it, Alex couldn't. His horses would never have made it twice. So then Olaf waited his chance and reported Alex and Alex was made to scatter his load. Such things happened, Dad says, feuds building up like that. In fact, it seems they were a morose, suspicious lot, those squatters back of the river. Maybe that's what starving does for you. That and being alone too much. The town, except for trading at the store, wouldn't have anything to do with them, and only a few of them were married.

"Opium in the Cough Syrup" could be the title of tonight's story. Dad had heard about Alex's troubles, so he'd gone out to Alex's place with some groceries and some meat he'd butchered himself. "Well boys," Dad was saying, "I ran into a helluva mess. There they were all huddled around the stove wearing every scrap of clothes they owned which wasn't much. That old homesteader's shack they were in, I tell you,there was spaces between the logs wide enough to swing a cat through. They had it all stuffed with hay and rags as best they could and it was pretty iced up. Still that rusted out stove was no match for that north wind."

It was one of those rare evenings for us, so warm we could sit outside without sweaters. I tried to imagine that other scene, being abandoned to a darkness in which death was a real possibility. If such thoughts were difficult for me, what were they like for Helen? The answer is, impossible. She got up and moved inside, brushing past me on her way to the telephone and television. I listened, my ear to the close warm dusk, giving myself up to the pleasure of Dad's tongue curling around his words.

"Alex was raving. Had been for five days, since getting back from town with an empty sleigh and nothing to show for it. The flu, Mavis thought it was, or maybe pneumonia. She had him on a cot, pulled in close to the stove. He was tossing and mumbling, mostly gibberish. Then every once in a while he'd sit straight up, sudden like, his eyes wide, and shout. You couldn't make head nor tail of it. Well, he was scaring the kids half to death. I'd thought to take along this cough syrup, and I poured the whole bottle in him. Well boys, after that he slept quiet as a baby. The wonder is he ever woke up. It wasn't until after I married your Gramma I realized what I'd done. She read the label on every damn thing. That was one thing about your Gramma."

This was the break I was waiting for. Brian's protests were merely a ritual. He knew the rules. But he sensed my impatience. He dawdled over brushing his teeth, put his pyjama bottoms on his top and stuck his arms through the legs, grinned at me. I did not smile. I wanted to get back to Dad. That was happening more and more, the feeling that I wanted to spend more time with him. I wanted to find out certain things. You'd think if I'd been listening to his stories all those years, I'd know everything. But the truth was Dad had always escaped me. I mean the real man behind the stories. Strange, how with Mother who revealed everything when she spoke, I found myself drawing back, but with Dad whose stories were a cover, I always wanted more.

When I got back to the patio with a tray of fresh coffee, cups and saucers, Dad was still talking abut Alex and Mavis. "Something has really gotten him on to them tonight," I thought. I couldn't see him clearly because it was nearly dark, but he was sitting in a lawn chair across from me. His head was lowered.

Dad was a very good looking man. He had a wonderful face, deep with experience, and a bush of grey hair and moustache. Maybe girls are always half in love with their fathers. My earliest memories are of climbing up on his knee, the way Brian did, of snuggling into his comforting smells, of feeling his strength. Dad was always there when I needed him. He always knew what to do. When I left the farm to come into the city to go to university, lonely and confused, I would phone home. It was Dad I would ask for. He could always cheer me up. Mother's manner destroyed me further. She left me feeling that my problems were real, whereas he made me see them as fabrications.

Dad taught me everything—to ride, to shoot, to pitch hay, to drive the tractor. I don't think he was trying to make a man of me. He wasn't like that. But I insisted on being with him all the time, so naturally he taught me his skills.

I poured coffee, put cream and sugar into Dad's, stirred it, passed it to him. He didn't see my hand or the cup. I set it down on the low table beside him. "Alex was out like a light," he said. "The rest of us were huddled there around the stove, eating some biscuits and goulash Mavis had cooked up from the groceries I'd brought, when Mavis leaned close to me and asked would I do her a favour.

" 'If I can,' I said.

" 'Two days ago,' she said, 'Alex got up and went out looking for something to eat. I couldn't stop him,' she said. 'He took his gun. He came back empty-handed. Since then,' she said, 'every once in a while in his raving, it comes out, something about a body out in the bush.'

"Well, there was lots of that. Lots of strange things happened then. There in that swamp nature was the law. And nature can kill a man so easy, easy as popping a flea between your fingers.

" 'We heard a shot,' she said.

" 'Could mean anything,' I said.

"Well, she wanted me to go out and have a look. She would of gone herself except she didn't have boots and the snow was a couple of feet deep on the level, four or five feet in drifts. I think what it was though, she was afraid of what she'd find, because later she went, tied some rags around her feet and went.

" 'Can't be far,' she said. 'He was too weak to go far.'

"When I was at the door, she whispered something else. How when Alex came home from town after being made to scatter his logs, how he was slamming things around, slamming his fists at the table, how he went out to chop wood and broke the axe handle out of sheer rage. 'You know his temper,' she said.

"So she pointed me in the right direction and off I go and sure enough, about two hundred yards from the house near a clump of willows, there's Olaf, his rifle still in his hand, a bullet through his skull, entered clean through the left eye."

Dad stopped speaking. I was thinking that I'd never heard that story before. Suddenly, I was frightened. I remembered something I had learned about old people. How, near the end, certain stories surface in much the same way the body does, the way a body gets rid of itself, liquids, refuse, flesh. How, near the end, old people have an obsession to say certain things, things they've held in for years, things that would be better left unsaid. I did not like hearing such stories. I always wished the other person would show greater control.

"That head was one hell of a mess," Dad said. "Black, blood crusted and frozen. But the worst was, the birds had got his tongue. Magpies'll do that."

I stood up, rattled the cups and saucers onto the tray, took the tray into the kitchen. I started unloading the dishwasher, clattering things as much as I could. But I could still hear him.

"It wasn't until the next day we could talk to Alex. He was out of his delirium by then, looking rougher than a dog's breakfast, but still in the land of the living. 'I saw something move,' he said, 'and thought, by God, it's an elk. I wasn't thinking straight,' he said.

"No one could mistake Olaf's red beard. And a shot like that is no accident. Mavis and me didn't say anything, but he must've caught a look between us.

" 'Anyway,' he said, 'the bastard deserved it.' Then, like in a dream he said, 'There he was. I couldn't believe my eyes. Right in my sights. Delivered.'

"Then a look came over his face. 'Who'll ever know anyway?' he said. And he looked at me, and I could see he didn't trust me worth a damn. Mavis must've seen it too. 'He's our friend,' she said.

"Well, then we had to decide what to do. Alex was all for getting out right away. 'By the time anyone finds him we'll be hundreds of miles from here,' was the way he was figuring it.

" 'Where will we go?' said Mavis. 'Where in all this world is there a place for us and the kids? Here, at least, there's the tamarack and some rabbits. And spring will come. There'll be fish then, and berries. We'll starve in the city.'

"Well, she was right and Alex knew it. But we had to do something with poor Olaf. You couldn't just leave him out there, carrion for the magpies and anything else that happened along with a liking for flesh, living or dead. And they couldn't stay in that cabin knowing the body was out there. And Mavis kept looking at her kids.

"So we went out again, the three of us this time. I didn't want Mavis there, but she wouldn't stay back. So, then, we rolled Olaf into the swamp."

I came to with a start and realized I'd been standing for I don't know how long, suspended above the half-emptied dishwasher. The voice had stopped. Good, I thought. Maybe it's not too late. Maybe we can forget this happened.

"We smoothed the snow back over him." The voice started again. "Like dirt over a grave. And he was never found. In spring, he must've melted right down into the swamp and then sunk in the mud. No one noticed he was gone. No one kept a census on that bunch.

"Times changed. The war came. All them drifters moved on, got jobs, joined the forces. After the war the swamp was drained, the land cleared. They put in the road. They cut down the Wimot Hill. You wouldn't know it was the same country. Hay growing to beat the band there now. Lots of moisture. It always snowed a lot back in there."

The heat of the day collected in the house, and I could only think, "Is it finished now?"

" 'I keep remembering the head,' Mavis told me later. I can still hear the way she said it. 'That bloody frozen smashed head. I see it in my dreams,' she said. 'It keeps coming out of the swamp toward me, mouth open, the black gaping hole, making terrible sounds, begging me to do something to help it.' She came to see me one afternoon, by herself. Something was happening to Alex, she said. He always did have a short fuse. But now he was more touchy than ever. 'I can't leave him,' she said, 'there's too much between us.' "

Dad's throat seemed blocked, but he did nothing to clear it. He spoke through sounds of strangulation.

"Then in spring, they up and left. Just like that. They stopped by my place on the way out. Mavis said they couldn't leave without saying good-bye. She came and found me where I was working out by the barn. Alex didn't get out of the wagon. Ever since that day, y'see, he couldn't look me in the eye. Not because of what he'd done, but because I knew about it. He kind of hated me me for that. We couldn't talk about it, y'see. It was too deep. Well, when a man can't talk he's beat. Alex always was a suspicious bastard. The way he figured it, I had something on him."

Silence, complete, deafening, came out of the darkness of the patio. Thank

God, I thought. I did not want to hear stories not meant for my ear. Then I realized what I was thanking God for. And I wanted it back—my father's strong, sure voice.

"I ran into Alex once." An uneasy whine, like that of a sick child, started. "Years later, right here in this city. Ran into him on the street. So he says I'll buy you a beer and I says okay. Well, we get to talking and one thing leads to another and he says come on home and say hello to the wife. Well, that was the sorriest thing I ever done. There was Mavis, all dirty and uncombed and the place filthy and smelling. I knew right away what it was. It was the drink, y'see. They'd taken to it, the both of them. Oh, she was a mess, marks and bruises all over her arms and face. Sometimes," the strange voice said, "I think I did her a terrible wrong."

The voice broke down further, into fragments, into attempts to locate threads: "I should have known what Alex was like... maybe I did... I can't re-member... he just didn't have it in him, y'see... and he always did have a mean streak... but I did think I was doing the best for her... I guess I thought... I don't know what I thought... it might've been better if I... oh, I don't know... I don't know... but I couldn't report him, a man doesn't report on another man like that... and Mavis and me couldn't've lived with that... but I don't know... maybe I should've done something different... if I had stuck by her..."

I remembered my father's skin, the way I had seen it shortly before that August evening, when he came out of the bathroom in his undershirt. The skin on his arms was white and soft, and the flesh soft and wobbly under-neath. I dismissed it at the time, but standing there with darkness closing around me, I knew they were an old man's arms. No. Not an old man's arms, an old woman's arms. All I could feel was repulsion. I reached out my arm and switched on the light.

"But how can you ever be sure?" The voice took up its wailing.

Throughout Dad's story, Dave had been saying yes, yes, as though deal-ing with a patient. Now he said, "I've found that what seems right at the time usually is right. It's just that looking back, the issue gets clouded. We don't remember certain facts that determined our decision." His voice was remarkably cool and certain.

But the other voice did not want answers or solutions. It only repeated questions, going around and around, without conviction.

My father was a feeble old man. He would be eighty in September. Perhaps he would be confined to his bed. Perhaps he would soil himself and spill food down his shirt front. I could already smell his new smell, stale skin and urine. Out there in the darkness, he waited for a word from me before going to bed. But I didn't go back out there that night. I couldn't. And I wondered about tomorrow. How would I be able to face him? How would I be able to live the necessary lies? How would we get through our remaining days?

It wasn't as difficult as I thought it might be. We survived, or at least I did. Dad died, but then he had lived long enough. Maybe too long. Now I wonder. Did I ever love him? If I did, I should have loved him through to the end. Not that I was ashamed of him. At the end, I felt nothing, so I could not be ashamed of him. The shame was mine. How could I have let myself be seduced by such a diseased old man?

How could I have let myself be seduced by a man whose tongue failed him, by a man who, in the end, could only mouth pitiful incoherent cries, by a man who could not finish his story, by a man who did not KNOW the ending?

## How I Spent My Summer Holidays

The Home squats obscenely in the middle of a field. Around us houses form a distant circle. This is after catastrophe and construction is beginning again. Still, no one dares this strip we walk on or the thing that sits like a raised boil at its centre.

In my mind now, as I sit amongst my bottles of blood, we cross and recross that no man's land of thistle and quackgrass. It must have been green sometimes, if only for a short while in the spring, but I always see it as brown and feel it as prickly. Endlessly, we trudge to and from school, eyes bent to the ground. We do not remember why we are here; our brains are seared bare as the landscape we move across.

Marlene speaks in her high whine. "What's wrong with you? What's wrong with a person like you anyways? Are you crazy or something?"

My response is silence.

"Why did you shout, 'I can't see, I can't see'?" Marlene shrills on. Then, disgusted, "You were weird."

"That's what happens when you faint." My foot deftly avoids a pile of dog shit which steers me toward a broken beer bottle. I swerve again.

Even though I have these explanations and the distinction of being the only kid in the Home with the experience of fainting, I feel inadequate, especially with Marlene. Marlene is the Wonder Woman of the Home. She has the biggest mouth and can hold water in it the longest, all the way from the toilet sink to where we crouch in the dirt by the playhouse.

We need this water for our brick dust pies. We are not allowed to take containers such as cups outside. Sometimes, someone finds a tin can. Then that person has something to bargain with and the rest of us watch with envy. We constantly sift through garbage for such treasures, but this is during rationing and short supply. To scrape the bricks, which we dig from the playhouse foundation, we use nails or shards of glass gleaned from rubble. After use, these are placed carefully on a special ledge. In spite of such restrictions, we construct our pies as best we can, and take pride in them, too, not having experienced how grand they might be with more sophisticated tools.

So we walk always watching the ground for broken or torn bits of string or metal. We walk together, seven or eight of us, the big kids. They do not tell us our ages but we do have grades at school. I am in grade five; Eddie is in grade six. If we raise our heads, we can see another group, the little kids, their dark outlines merging into one shape.

Eddie speaks. He is the one who always comes to my rescue. "What *you* should be saying," he says to Marlene, "is 'I can't find my brain.'"

We walk slowly. We do not want to arrive. Constantly, we are aware of the thing in front of us, three stories, red brick, wooden verandah. Inner boundaries are only half-heartedly established, a caragana hedge at the front, a wire fence along the playground side, three strands of barbed wire along the garden side. These aren't necessary, because no one ever wants to get in, and the difficulties of getting out have nothing to do with wire fences. We are told that no one has escaped. What they mean is escapees are always found, sleeping in the bus depot or lifting something from Woolworth's.

Eddie and Ray often go out at night, just to be free, they say. They take in a movie or watch the drunks on 97th Street. They always have money. Possibly they roll those bodies that lie limp in alleys and doorways. They always return because where else is there to go? They speak of adventure, but then everybody here tells lies, especially when faced with authority. We'll say anything to save ourselves. But when they get caught escaping, there is nothing they can say. Then, it's the strap for sure. Mr. Epsom does the boys. But that isn't why Eddie hates him.

Mr. Epsom is supposed to be the gardener, but he only got the job because of Mrs. Epsom who is the cook and saves the Board piles of money with hot water she calls soup and cold water with bits of floating bread she calls pudding. As to the gardening, the kids do most if it, while

Mr. Epsom shuffles around with his evil eye. The kids, naturally, don't do any more than they have to, which is why the marigolds are always rusty and the grass splotchy, worn to the dirt in some places, overgrown in others.

In looks the Epsoms are the tall and short, the lean and fat. She is bustly and minds her own business, especially where the Board and the Head are concerned. Her biggest job is keeping Mr. Epsom on the straight, scrubbed and pruned. But sometimes he gets away from her. Once a week he has his Legion night, and then if you stay awake long enough you can spot him from the dorm window, weaving his way across the field. You can hear him fumbling for the gate latch and swearing to himself.

Everyone at the Home knows certain facts of survival. No one speaks of these things. They are transferred amongst us by a process something like osmosis. We know how to sneak down the fire escape; we know to try and get a kitchen job because then you can give yourself the biggest helpings of what you like and the smallest of what you don't; we know to watch out for Mr. Epsom. We know to stay away from the garden shed because that is where he keeps his dirty pictures and sits playing with himself.

All this isn't why Eddie hates Mr. Epsom, though. The reason Eddie hates him is because Mr. Epsom is the one who hacked Mr. McGregor to bits.

The voices come again. As I push yet another needle into a vein raised blue and irresistible beneath the skin, I hear Eddie's long drawn-out 'hey' full of admiration and wonder. I see Mr. McGregor coiled and sunning himself in the field, except at first I do not see him. What I see is his movement near my foot as he whips open in a shimmer of light. I have no picture of my reaction. As my psychologist friend would say, I've probably repressed it.

Right away, Eddie picks him up.

"What if he's poison," says Marlene.

Eddie doesn't care. He would rather die than not touch him.

"Garter," says someone.

"Rattler," says another.

"None of those," says Ray, who's an Indian and knows.

"What then?"

"I dunno," says Ray. "I never saw one of them before."

All the rest of the way that snake curls up and down Eddie's arms. He's about four feet long, greyish beige with patches of rust. He holds onto

Eddie's arm so tightly we can't get our fingers in beneath the two skins. We take turns trying. At first I won't do it. I don't want to touch anything cold and slimy. But I can feel Marlene's appraising eyes, her eagerness to tell the world about my cowardice. As it turns out, Mr. McGregor is smooth and soft and warm from the sun. He is incredibly strong, his body a thick, hard muscle, frightening because of the way it has its own life and can turn so quickly. Eddie calls him "he" but Mr. McGregor's delicate face and black tongue furling out so gracefully make me think of Lily.

Lily of the almond eyes and toffee skin. Lily with holes in her ears threaded with finely spun gold. One recess she tells me she is twelve, her birthday is February nineteenth. She tells me she is Hungarian. I detect a slight accent.

I go home with her once, even though it is against the rules. It means starvation and solitary but it is worth it, if only for the smells, cinnamon, other spices I do not recognize. In the kitchen a grandmother with jiggly arms rolls dough. Milk, icy and creamy, foams up out of tall glasses. Cookies, row upon row, cool on wire racks. A strange language, quick, fierce, loving, is spoken without effort. On the wall a clock ticks. I thought school was the only place with clocks.

In the living room it doesn't seem to matter if Lily touches things or sits in the chairs. She shows me glass figurines like jewels and painted wooden dolls, each fitting perfectly inside the others, each with a mouth in the shape of a heart. Upstairs, in her bedroom Lily sleeps alone in a bed that has four pillars and an umbrella. A closet is full of dresses, any colour you can think of. I touch everything, the pebbly bedspread, the wiry doll's hair. A white rug lies on the floor beside the bed. I take off one shoe and sock and put my foot into its soft thickness. On the bedside table there is another clock, this one made of pink shells.

At the Home we know time through Roxy. She is the one who calls us to stand in lines, for wash up, for meals. She tells us when to leave for school and when to go to bed. Roxy is scrawny as a mauled cow. She struts around on turned out ankles and worn down heels, waving a long stick and shouting. "Okay, everybody to their lockers!"

These doorless lockers line the playroom. In the past we must have each been assigned one. Sometimes, I think I spend my whole childhood sitting in mine, staring at nothing, memorizing the details of my teeth.

I *have* to start at the top left molars, inside. I work my way across the smooth surface to the extreme right edge, then return to the bottom inside left. Then I do the same with the outside, first top, then bottom. I work my tongue slowly; time is no object. There is something about their slipperiness, their solid feel, that I like. Outside in the playground, I often perform the same sort of ceremony with stones. I pop one into my mouth and roll it around and around with my tongue. My psychologist friend calls this repetition compulsion.

Returning, too, she says, to a place you once knew.

And I do wonder why I do this, return to this void where I feel such discomfort. In my more penetrating moments, I know I go back to try and change things, but I also know nothing can be changed. Why repeat? The terrible need to have things come out right.

And so again during the endless heat of that summer, Eddie scrounges alleys for chicken wire and builds a pen for Mr. McGregor down beyond the garden. A line of scraggly trees and overgrown shrubs make this the only place on the compound where you can not be seen, even from third floor windows. There's a shallow ditch where we sit and smoke and read comics. It must be nearly summer holidays when we find Mr. McGregor, because I spend long days down there watching Eddie clean the pen, watching Mr. McGregor curl himself like bracelets around Eddie's arms. I can never bring myself to let him do that to me, although part of me wants to.

Mr. McGregor is both beautiful and horrible. I mean in the way he takes his food. Eddie catches mice and gophers in the field. He lets them go into the pen, and Mr. McGregor squeezes them and swallows them whole, then goes off into a corner for three days to sleep it off. At first a big lump rounds out his stomach. You can see this get smaller and smaller. Then you know he needs to eat again.

I cannot stand watching. One quick squeeze would not be so bad. But it takes a few. At each squeeze, ,the victim lets out air until finally there is no space left for air to go in. As I sit in the playroom or spoon tapioca into twenty-seven sherbets lined up on the kitchen counter, I do not think about what is happening down in the garden. I do not think of the way the mouse scurries and the final frozen look on its face.

Otherwise, I'm with Eddie every chance I get. When I finish in the kitchen, I slip away and across the short space of grass. I can feel eyes watching me from behind, Mrs. Epsom maybe, or maybe the Head in his office. I try to become invisible.

As I go along the path, I meet Mr. Epsom. I shrivel myself and move around him. I keep my head down and try not to let anything bounce. Even if I don't actually meet him on this journey, I'm aware of him, his shadow in the yard or garden, or waiting in his shed. I think of him looking at his pictures. I turn sharply and walk quickly. I control my legs so they will not run.

"What's wrong with you?" Eddie asks when I arrive. "You're not going to faint are you?"

When Mr. Epsom catches me, though, it is in the kitchen, where I do not expect it. For one thing, Mrs. Epsom is usually there. But also, the kitchen is large and airy and white. Windows on two sides let in lots of light. There isn't a speck of dirt or a drip of food anywhere, not if Mrs. Epsom can help it. When I hear the screen door close and look up to see Mr. Epsom, my mind instinctively reaches for Mrs. Epsom, but she has gone to consult with the Head. My chest tightens. I keep my eyes on the eternal tapioca, glassy fish eggs in grey blue.

Mr. Epsom sits down on the bench near where I'm standing. I am wearing shorts Roxy gave me from the communal clothes cupboard and about two sizes too small. On my bare leg, I feel something wet, something being moved up and down, being stroked along skin, leaving a trail of wetness. This is a situation I can not think about. Although the room is starting to turn about me, I keep spooning out tapioca.

Mrs. Epsom is the one who saves me. The instant she barges in through the swinging door from the dining room, the thing on my leg disappears. In a matter of seconds, Mr. Epsom is gone. Mrs. Epsom looks at me, at my legs, and says something about young girls who run around half-naked. I feel queasy and unclean. Why did I not move to the other side of the table? Why did I not escape through the door? There is something wrong with me, something that forces me to submit, something that will not let me defend myself. And Mr. Epsom knows. After that, I live in terror. As long as Mr. Epsom is around, I am in danger, so when Eddie suggests getting rid of him, I'm all for it.

We are kneeling in the grass staring down at the bloody remains of Mr. McGregor. Mr. Epsom, shovel in hand, is heading back towards his shed mumbling something like, "Don't want no goddamn giant worm. Get rid-da that chicken wire, too," he growls across his shoulder. "Too much goddamn junk around this place."

I can see the tears just back of Eddie's eyes. "What I'm gonna do," he says through clenched teeth, "I'm gonna get ridda him."

"How?" I ask. "How?"

At first Eddie talks of hacking up Mr. Epsom so he can see what it's like. Next day, he decides it will be more subtle, not so much chance of getting caught, to simply give him a push at the top of the stairs. The trouble with this is Eddie lacks occasion. He never comes upon Mr. Epsom at the top of a suitably long flight of stairs. Finally, he settles upon scaring him to death.

We paint ourselves all over, faces, legs, arms, with this special paint that glows in the dark. We smear it on some clothes we got from the rag cupboard. We glue our hair so it sticks straight up. We paint gashes and holes with blood dripping out of them all over our faces. We stick feathers and fur on our bodies. One thing about Eddie, he can get anything, just don't ask any questions.

We hide in the caragana hedge on Legion night and wait for Mr. Epsom to come home drunker than a hoot owl. "He'll think we're his DT's, larger than life," says Eddie with satisfaction.

The night is dark. Skinny fingers of clouds cover most of the moon. We wait, crouched, not daring to look at each other, scarcely daring to breathe. We hear something at the gate and Mr. Epsom going through his list of curse words. We hear his footsteps coming closer. Then, it cannot be more perfect. Just as we leap into his path, arms raised, mouths wide in silent screams, tongues stretched to our chins, the clouds blow across the moon.

There we are in all our glory, in the spotlight. Mr. Epsom stops. His eyes bug out. He does a little dance, first one way then the other. He catches himself, balances on one foot, lurches toward us with his arms outstretched. His hands go for our throats. We step aside. His face twists. It is a strange colour. He staggers past us, then backward again, then forward, then sideways.

We watch until the final pitch into his own bed of drooping petunias. Then, we move fast. We do not look back. Next morning at breakfast comes the solemn announcement. Mr. Epsom has passed away in the night. The gossip is poison. Where he got it is a mystery. Someone says moonshine, someone says chicken, someone says Mrs. Epsom's cooking.

When I hear the word poison, I can only repeat to myself thank you, thank you, thank you, to some invisible decision-maker who lifted the whole thing out of my irresponsible hands. Eddie, however, is disappointed. We are in the smoking ditch, hiding from the sun. "We didn't do nothing," he says. "It wasn't us at all. We thought we looked shit hot. Some great Hollywood production, when all the time we were just a couple of kids with a feather or two and some paint. Pitiful." His voice is angry. At first

I think he is angry with me, or Mr. Epsom. Then I realize he is angry with himself.

Patsy Arnold gave me the farm idea. She sat directly in front of me. Already, she was busy writing. I stared at the back of her head. Then it happened, the miracle. The flecks of white scalp showing between those tight French braids transported me. There was something, too, about the braids themselves, the perfection of the way they were woven, the taut hairs held in marvellous tension. Probably, it also had something to do with Patsy's stories before morning bell.

Patsy had a million relatives, all on farms. She had uncles and aunts, grandmothers and grandfathers, first cousins, second cousins, third cousins. She had relatives I had never even heard of. "Second cousin once removed," she recited in a high piping voice. Her mother came from a family of thirteen, her father from a family of eleven. My mind boggled. She related family picnics, weddings, family ball games. I was left gasping. She spoke of driving tractors, running with dogs, riding horses. She may as well have been talking about riding balloons beyond the clouds.

The problem was I could not tell the truth. The truth was I had done nothing during the summer. How could I talk about dishing out tapioca, picking raspberries, sitting in my locker, making brick dust pies? It was too shameful.

The teacher told us to take our stories home for homework and bring them back the next morning. All that evening I sat in the toilet writing. It was quieter than the playroom. Once I got started I couldn't stop. It was crazy. The lies compounded so easily. I told things I didn't even know I knew. I told about my non-existent grandmother who kept forgetting things like where she was and where she had left her teeth. I revealed my imagined aunt's moustache—fine dark hairs springing out of pulsating pores just above moist lips, drooping down to faint fleshy jowls, soft and alive.

Where my words came from is a mystery. Perhaps they were of another life that I could not remember. Perhaps they were inside me, lying waiting. All I know is, as I scribbled furiously on, they possessed me. They told a story of sounds and smells and visions, bells echoing, hay freshly cut. Horses in impossible green pastures suddenly become possible. Dogs barked in air so pure it shone as with a white light. They ran, they jumped, they twisted bodies so sleek that the words *copper* and *satin* took on new meanings.

But I have to admit my forte was people. I assumed so easily the story of my fabricated uncle's toenails: he always cut his toenails in the living room, which my aunt said was uncouth. One day, my little boy cousin crawling around on the floor was seen to be chewing something which turned out to be my uncle's toenail, and my aunt really screamed at my uncle, but he hollered back that toenails would make a man of him. "If it's toenails you want, kid," he said, "there's lots more where them came from. I'll start saving em up for you!"

When I was finished, I read it over. There was something wrong. It lacked romance. That was where Clarabelle came in. She was my cousin who was tragically in love with this guy my uncle couldn't stand who worked on the oil rigs and walked around town with his boots and his leather jacket open. On Saturday night coming home from the dance their car went off the road, which was like grease because of the rain, and they didn't get home until morning and there was a terrible row with my uncle shouting and waving his fists and my cousin wringing her hands and crying and saying what had she done so wrong anyway, all they did was sleep in the ditch.

Somewhere in the distance Roxy was shouting. I had forgotten about Roxy and the cubicle in which I sat, its cement floor, its leaky pipes, its damp odours. The call was for bed and lights out. I had to stop writing, but my fingers refused to stop twitching. For hours I kept leaping up in the darkness to find my scribbler, to kneel in the moonlight at the foot of my bed, to add, to correct, to delete.

The next day I did not want to abandon my composition to the immaculate hands of Adelaide. Adelaide was the person for whom I reserved a special contempt. She dotted all her i's and crossed all her t's. She always collected papers and handed out pencils and got out early on days we reviewed test papers. When that perfect hand was stuck in front of my face, a hand so clean you could see into every white pore, I suddenly knew that my story was not acceptable. It contained the sweaty imprints of my hand, the wrinkles of that impossible position perched on the toilet edge having to make hurried exits when someone knocked on the door calling was I going to be there all night and maybe a dose of castor oil would fix me up.

There was something else too, something about betraying my relatives to people like Adelaide, people who would not understand them. But I had no choice. I gave them over. A couple of days later when the papers were returned, mine wasn't among them. Disaster hung heavy over my head. Had I been lost? Or simply forgotten? Or perhaps mine had been so bad the teacher had thrown it, in disgust, into the waste paper basket.

Then I heard my name and could I stay at recess. This was having the accusatory finger pointed. My lies must have been discovered. This was calamity.

At recess, as I approached the teacher's desk, I saw my story in all its defects, lying exposed on top of a pile of other papers. It looked even grubbier than I remembered. Red pencil marks were all over it, like my face with measles. Angry scratches crossed out whole paragraphs.

I'll never forget the teacher's fingernails, so squarely pruned, so highly buffed, the cuticles so precise. By the end of that session, I had memorized them. I was right about the lies. How could I have been so dumb? Of course, all the teachers knew the Home kids. It was down in their registers. And even if it wasn't, all you had to do was look at us. We all had the same haircut, straight bangs, straight around the bottom edge. You could tell by our clothes, every year the same ones, only on different bodies. You could tell by the impetigo scabs and the ever-present smell of seven-year itch powder.

"There's nothing wrong with writing a story," the teacher's voice said, "as long as we don't pretend it's the truth." Then she couldn't resist the question. "You do know, don't you, that this isn't real? It's important to keep things separate, in our own minds, that is."

I said nothing. After a moment, her voice changed gear. She started talking about my story being well done, in a way. She talked about some sort of writing competition for young Canadians. She said how my story was too long and how it needed some style and some smoothing over. She said she would show me how to do this. She gave me a note so I could stay after school the next day. I can see now that what we did to that story was tone it down a couple of notches. We didn't exactly remove my uncle's temper and Clarabelle's ditch romance but we subdued them. And what we did to the spelling and grammar was out of this world. By the time we were finished, I scarcely recognized myself at all.

I didn't in a prize, but I got honourable mention. All the winners plus the honourable mentions got put into the newspaper, one every week, on the Satruday Children's page. Mine didn't come up for several weeks, and I never saw it anyway because we never got to look at a paper. I know it appeared, though, because the Monday morning after, the teacher said did I like seeing it and my name in print and I said yes.

I thought that was the end of it, but I was doomed to be haunted by that story. A few months later, it was winter because I remember the caragana hedge as bare twisted branches growing out of the Head sitting in front of the window, Roxy told me I was wanted upstairs. Upstairs did not mean the kitchen, the dining room, or the dormitories, which were all, also, upstairs. It meant the *Office* with everything contained in that word.

Sometimes, kids returned from the office looking like torture victims, their faces numb, their bodies moving like sleepwalkers. Sometimes, kids would disappear into the office never to be seen or heard of again. Occasionally it was good news, a visitor, especially good if the visitor brought candy. But sometimes the call came because a kid had done something so bad it was beyond Roxy's stick. So it was with mixed looks of envy and relief that the other kids watched me walk past them and start up the steps.

It was more terrible than I could have imagined. I was faced with my lies. My characters had come to life. There was an aunt with a moustache, there was a blustery uncle, I could only assume he had toenails, there was even a cousin called Clarabelle. They were all there, in pulsating flesh. Even before anyone spoke, I was struck by dismay at what I had done. These were my people. I had created them. Yet they were unfamiliar and definitely unfriendly.

Now, as I watch another vein collapse and another vial fill with purplish blood, I hear their voices, full of accusation and denial, come at me again in a clamouring rush.

My uncle: "How could you do this to us, smear us all over the paper like that?"

My cousin: "Making us sound like hicks."

My aunt: "My house never looked like that. I keep my house clean as anybody."

My cousin advances, head high, pointing at her chin. "You call that a double chin? Ah!" She turns away in disgust. "You don't even know what a double chin is!" This is in regard to a slight descriptive reference in which I was only trying to give her a unique appearance.

My aunt speaks of spite and my uncle of suing if I weren't a child.

After a long and stunning trial came the sentence delivered by the Head, a blank skull shape against a square of light. The voice was detached. It seemed to descend from the ceiling. "What's done is done. The best we can do now is an apology and a promise that this will never happen again."

I so apologized and promised, my words echoing those of the Head. Then I slunk away, back downstairs, and went and sat in my locker. I thought about things. How could I have done that? How could I have told the truth when I did't know what it was? Maybe I had some special power. I thought of Mr. Epsom. Maybe it had not been poison. Maybe if I could make people live, I could also make them die. This was too horrible to think about for long. I made a solemn vow to myself to stop sticking pins in dolls. Never, never again would I chant magic formulas of either life or death. Such acts, even such thought of such acts, are too dangerous.

Eddie builds a snow cave in the ditch. A tarp covers the floor where we sit. It is warm and cozy and peaceful in that hollow white space alone with Eddie. We are half-way through a bottle of scotch, another one of Eddie's finds. Now the taste of scotch rises up in me and threatens my system. But then I am where I want to be, with Eddie. He takes a long pull on his cigarette and draws the smoke deep into his lungs. I watch in admiration. I never inhale; I would pass out. Eddie speaks, "That's what you gotta learn, that's what you gotta remember. There's no relief, no miracles." His voice is already dead.

Would it have made a difference if I had been able to tell him about magic? But then how could I? I had already turned away from belief. Once, from some vague source, I heard how Eddie made out later, on the outside. He did a lot of breaking and entering, aggravated assault, drug selling. I heard he died of an overdose, methadone, which he gave to himself, but I can't remember where I heard it.

None of this is true. Or some of it may be true. But I never brought people to life. I never killed people. I'm not that powerful or dangerous. Sometimes, I think I make up everything. Years ago, I began to suspect myself. I began to wonder about hearing that gate latch, about waiting, shivering in the hedge, about the sound and feel of those footsteps coming closer. I began to suspect I was dreaming, that the picture I have in my mind of Mr. Epsom falling is from something else, something I have read, maybe. I began to wonder if Eddie and I dressed up and hid in the hedge at all. It seems to me now that I dreamed up this story after the announcement of Mr. Epsom's death. But did Mr. Epsom ever live?

Why then do these voices haunt me? These people cannot come to life and accuse me, Marlene of her big mouth, Mr. Epsom of his evil ways. And Eddie. How can he accuse me of not giving him what he needed? And how can I get caught up in my own fictions, to think it matters?

I find the safest thing to do is simply go on with my blood-letting. This I can be sure is real—my white uniform, my sterile instruments, the spotless counters, the glistening vinyl. And at the end of a good day's work, as I close the door on the small room they allow me in this place, I feel a satisfied glow seeing my vials of blood, all sitting neatly in racks along the wall, all tagged and labelled with black ink.

## Windstorm

Conversations with my mother are starting to sound like the obituary column. Every time we go out to see her and Dad in Hackett or they come into Calgary, it's the same old story. Only the names change.

"Well, poor Bert Norris went last week," she'll say, pushing back from the lunch table and blotting the corners of her mouth with a paper napkin.

The boys have run off to play, and Walter's at work even though it's Saturday. Since he got his own oil field supply business he works all the time. Dad had wandered off to watch TV, mostly because he likes the wrestling but also because he doesn't like to listen to mother's stories. "Get to the point, woman," he'll exclaim without raising his voice, changing the shape of words not by inflection but by the force of his presence.

Anyway, I'm concentrating on shaving pablum from the baby's chin, and it takes me a minute to place in context either Bert Norris or the ominous tone of the word *went*. Went? Went where, I want to say.

It's always the same. She tosses these names at me when the phone and the door are both ringing, Greg brings in an army of friends for kool-aid, and Barry has just overturned the can of Mazola onto the kitchen floor. "You remember Kate Metcalfe?" she shouts from the other side of the pass-through counter. I shuffle through my mental file cards and come up with the spinster music teacher, her thin aristocratic nose and her tuning fork humming in the white light of a hundred winter school rooms smelling of wet rubber boots and orange peels.

Miss Metcalfe was English. Because she was from the outside, our group, the girls of the whispered cloakroom consultation, naturally found her interesting enough to fabricate her history. We made her out to be a tragic figure. For us, anyone who didn't manage to get married was a tragic figure, but for Miss Metcalfe we contrived an especially sad, long ago, fatal love affair, the word *affair* having far more innocent connotations then than now.

"A young woman like that," Mother shakes her head. Anyone below sixty-five is young to her. Apparently, Kate Metcalfe had a stroke right in the middle of the Red & White on Saturday afternoon. She was shopping for groceries the way she had every Saturday afternoon for thirty years. And then *this* had to happen. "We played bridge together Friday evening!" Mother fairly shrieks her disbelief.

Sudden deaths for her are the worst. She can deal better with the ones that she can see coming, that seem to be logical outcomes of events, that almost seemed to be planned by the deceased. "You don't go until you're ready," she'll often say. She feels that many times she has predicted death. So-and-so is losing heart, is the way she might put it. Often, she doesn't reveal such predictions until after the event, but according to her that does not make them any less valid.

It's when things take a sudden unexpected twist that Mother's imagination catches hold like a leech and feeds itself to distraction. "So hard to believe," she shakes her head, dazed. "So hard to believe." For this reason she had a particularly difficult time with my cousin Francie's death. She didn't want to think that something could just swing down out of the sky like that and carry a person away, like a hawk will a mouse. Although, being a prairie person, you'd think she'd be used to the unexpected, especially when it comes in the form of weather.

To be specific, in Francie's case, it was a tornado. The people out there say cyclone. Hackett is near the Alberta-Saskatchewan border, and tornadoes aren't all that unusual there. They come up from the midwest States. Maybe you've read about the famous cyclone of 1912 that flattened Regina. It killed several people and did millions of dollars worth of damage when that was a lot of money. I, myself, remember small tornadoes that picked up a fence or a pile of hay, maybe the odd chicken. And then there were the ones that never set down, that just rode high enough above ground that they didn't catch anything but scared you all the same because you never knew for sure what they were going to do.

I remember Dad watching those ones, the way they'd hover in the distance against that huge sky, hover like flying saucers, closing in with their shadows, then passing over, leaving the sky blue and clear again and the August heat hanging. Dad would continue with his swathing, or whatever, right through it, but would always keep track of it, where it was and in what direction it was moving.

Only once did I see him roused by that cone shape, and then it wasn't the shape itself but the colour of the sky and the smell of the air. It was a typical day for cyclones, starting out hot and muggy and still, and it was August, the best, or worst, time. I remember the heat especially, because I was helping Mother can green beans, not exactly a volunteer situation. I was in high school then. I envied my town friends who were allowed to get jobs while I worked like a slave all summer for nothing. Anyway, it must have been over a hundred in that kitchen. Why Mother decided to can beans on a day like that, I'll never know, and I probably said as much to her. But I didn't need to ask. I knew the answer. It was the answer to everything on the farm. "The beans won't wait." The cows won't wait; the light won't wait. I'd been hearing it all my life.

Anyway, we were so busy we didn't notice what was happening outside. But then the kitchen suddenly got dark. Through the window we could see that the southern sky was an olive green colour. The funny thing was the living room on the north side of the house was still bright with unsuspecting sunlight. When we went outside, we could see the dark closing over the light, like the slow close of an eyelid shutting out day, shutting us into a nightmare where the air was copper. It was eerie, like being on the moon or something, where nothing could live because of the strange, totally hostile atmosphere.

Dad drove into the yard. He had been working out in the field. He stepped down from the truck, went into the shed, came out with a roll of binder twine. He told my brother Henry to take care of the pigs and chickens. He told me to gather up everything that was loose, wheelbarrows, forks, pails, into the barn. What I noticed was his directions were definite and precise. His movements were not especially hurried. The way his thick fingers tied a knot seemed almost leisurely. But he never had to do anything twice. He never retraced his steps. It seemed strange to me that he wasn't more excited. Because by then the whole sky was the colour of mud with a greenish oil slick across it, and I knew that something terrible was going to come out of that dark, boiling ocean.

In the house Mother and my sister had made sandwiches and filled ther-
moses with tea. They were taking this down to the basement. Heaped
in a pile on the floor by the steps were some sweaters and coats, the
idea of which a half-hour ago would have been ridiculous. But it had turned so cold I had goose bumps all over my arms. When Dad told Henry
to get the Coleman lamp and the first aid kit, it suddenly struck me what
this was all for. We would go down there, below the ground, and there
was a possibility, say if the house was flattened on top of us, that we'd
be trapped down there for several hours, until we could either dig ourselves
out or the Hackett Civil Defense made it to our place. For most people
that would be preferable to facing a tornado but as for me, I would rather
take my chances above ground. That's because ever since I was five years
old I've suffered from claustrophobia.

Maybe I even had it before then. But that's when I found out about
it, one Sunday afternoon when the Harleys dropped in for a visit. As usual
the kids went outside, and someone got the bright idea of this game where
you take turns tossing each other in a blanket. There were three Harleys,
two boys and a girl, my brother and sister, and me. Somehow, when it
was my turn to get tossed the blanket got twisted around me. I couldn't
get out. Of course, the others paid no attention to my screams. They
didn't recognize them as screams of terror, but if they had, likely it would
only have made the game more fun. It was my sister who, being older
with maybe a little more sense, finally decided that something was not
quite right. Even so, the blanket was so tight it took them another minute
or two to untangle it. That minute of life, or death, was a hundred years
in my time scheme. And I'll never forget that first breath of freedom.

So that was why I heard my voice saying to Dad, "I can't."

He was standing with his hand on the radio dial, but all he could get
was static so he clicked it off. "Well," he said, "what do you suggest we do?"

My brain was wild, bouncing off impossible solutions. "We could leave.
Just get in the car and leave. Just drive away from this place." I couldn't
look at his eyes. I looked at his mouth.

It opened. I'm sure he meant to say something like, "What kind of damn
fool notion is that?" But then he closed it. I guess he realized he had a
panic-stricken filly on his hands. So he did the same with me he would
do with it. He touched me. He placed his big, beefy, calloused hand around
my arm and let me feel his strength. He spoke to me quietly. His eyes
were steady. Mine were flitting around like birds caught in the house.

"Likely," he said, "likely it'll turn out to be nothing more than a storm." Right then, a wave of thunder broke and shattered around our ears. The lights went out.

To make a long story short, it did turn out to be only a bad storm. I use the word *only* in a relative sense, because there was still a lot of damage done that day. And all we could do was stand at various windows watching. The weather vane on top of the barn whirled crazily like a spinning top. The chicken coop chimney was torn off and carried away. The willows were bent to the ground and whipped sharply back up. Several of the branches were snapped clean and were whisked away. Down by the machine shed a four by four fence post was sheared off at ground level as neatly as though it were cut through with a saw. The fence on either side toppled. The slats sailed past the window. You could actually hear the scream of wood and nails being wrenched apart as the shed door took wings. The air was full of dirt, chaff, small branches. Not only was there our own debris, but other bits and pieces the wind had picked up miles away and, in fits and starts, laid down and picked up again. A pile of wired slats that none of us recognized was dumped near the back gate. For a few moments it lay there like a heap of broken bones, then once more it became airborne northwest. And that was only the wind. Then came the rain and the hail.

Sometime, in the middle of all this, I turned around and there was Mother sitting in the big chair by the kitchen stove in the almost-dark, reading. As for Dad, he stood—barrel chest out, hands pushed into back pockets, feet braced—first at one window, then another. Now I could see that he was probably mentally preparing his list. The fence would have to be fixed. The machine shed roof reshingled. One thing about Dad, when the storm was over it was over. He did not waste time on might-have-beens. Life for him consisted of the next thing on the list, whether it was mowing the south field or walking down that long church aisle with me on his arm. He's still like this. The truth is that Dad, bless his heart, has no imagination. He thinks in terms of actualities rather than possibilities. This allows a certain stance toward life that people mistake as courage. And if you think courage is facing difficulty or danger without fear, then he is courageous. But if you stop and think about it, facing things with fear requires more courage. Anyway, take it from me, a person like Dad can be a real stabilizing force for flibbertigibbets, which brings me to Mother.

When traits were handed out in that great warehouse in the sky, Mother must have by mistake gotten a double portion of imagination, maybe Dad's. This means she always has something on the burner in the way of a worry. When one fades into the background (they never really get solved) she simply grabs another. You might say she has her own kind of list. People like Mother should never hear about the insect in Africa that burrows under your skin and works its way to your brain and slowly eats it. When Mother heard that story she went pale and shuddered and said how no one would ever get her to go to Africa, not in a million years. A person like Mother should never read the doctor's column in the paper, because she'll lie awake at night convinced she has periarteritis nodosa which she was perfectly safe from until it entered her imagination. Anyway, the reason I'm bringing up this subject of Mother's imagination is that it's what makes the telling of Francie's story confused.

It happened last summer, the early part of summer, June. All the facts were in the Calgary paper. Francie made the front page. "Hackett woman killed by tornado." The story told how, apparently, she was lifted right out of her kitchen and let go half a mile away in a grain field. The amazing thing was that one of her kids, he'd be my cousin once removed, everybody calls him Bobby which he hates and wants to be called Rob, anyway Bobby was home at the time. He was in the very next room and didn't know a thing about what happened to his mother until he went to the kitchen to get something to eat. Or tried to go to the kitchen. He couldn't actually go to it because it wasn't there any more.

When I read that I thought they must have got it wrong. But later Dad told me it was true. I should explain that their house is, or was, in the shape of an L, and the kitchen, a lean-to addition, stuck out. The way the tornado set down and lifted, it just ripped off that lean-to. I saw pictures of it later and the walls connecting the kitchen to the house were still there. It seemed so strange, the way, in its dance, that thing just lighted a moment for Francie. Well, to be honest it did get some machinery and a couple of sheds too, but mainly it got Francie.

The other unbelievable thing was that Bobby hadn't heard anything. But then Dad explained how he had the stereo going and his headset on and Bobby himself told me how he always listens to his music lying down on the floor with his eyes closed. So, in the end, I got a logical explanation for it all, or most of it.

At the time, I phoned my parents right away. I wanted to make sure they were all right. Also, I wanted to know more about Francie. When

I talked with Mother she seemed hesitant to say anything. She did a lot of hinting, but I couldn't tell at what. Then Dad took the phone and said how it was all a lot of damn foolishness. "What's a lot of damn foolishness?" I shouted into the receiver.

"As usual," he said, "your Mother is letting herself get carried away."

I didn't have a chance to really talk to my parents until August. Every summer, the kids and I go out to Hackett. Walter drives us out, stays a couple of days, then gets back to his business. In two weeks, we repeat the procedure only in reverse.

We arrived about mid-morning, and I could hardly wait until the day was over, the kids bathed and tucked into bed, so at last I could talk with Mother. Usually Walter and Dad sit in the living room and drink beér and Mother and I sit in the kitchen and drink coffee. But that evening Dad insisted on sitting in the kitchen with us, because as he said, he knew what we were going to talk about and he wanted to make damn sure Mother got it straight for once.

"Why don't we go out and sit on the patio?" Mother turned to me with the manner of someone absolutely struck by her own brilliance. I should mention that my parents live right in the town of Hackett since Dad retired a few years ago and let Henry run the farm. They have a new house in the latest development on the edge. Looking out their kitchen window you can see virtually unlimited space, grain fields stretching unbroken to the horizon. When they moved there Dad built a fence. All the houses in that row have fences, as though the owners are trying to define and control a segment of space for themselves. The fences are sturdy, most-ly 1x6's, with stout posts and rails. Some of them are picketed along the top edge. Still, somehow, they don't convince. There's simply too much on the other side of the scale.

The reason my parents chose a house in that area has nothing to do with space and everything to do with the covetousness of farm women of Mother's generation for what is new and clean. Having lived so long in an old house with old furniture, old linoleum, old wood stove converted to electricity, Mother wanted everything to be spanking new. So they bought a brand new house and brand new everything else and left the old to Henry and his wife.

As far as nature is concerned, Dad thinks of it in terms of work and, like most men who have spent their lives outside, would rather be inside. That is why Mother suggested the patio, besides the fact that she likes to say the word. She knew that Dad would mumble something about mosquitoes and damn country anyway and head for the TV. But he did not. He simply picked up his beer and followed us. It was then that I really became curious. What, in God's name, was Mother about to tell me?

Francie was my cousin by marriage, being married to my cousin Stan. I have never really known Stan. He's ten years older than I, so we didn't go to school together or hang around the café or Saturday night dances during the same years. In 1960, when he brought a new wife back from Calgary and settled her in on the family farm, I was twelve with my own unique set of problems.

She was from England, one of those energetic sparkling English girls who set out to see the world. Stan met her at a party in Calgary. He soon got tired of driving 150 miles to see her, so they didn't have a very long courtship. I got these details from supper-table talk.

The first time I actually saw Francie was at the community shower held for her in the United Church basement. Mother was on the food committee at the time. It seems to me as long as I can remember Mother has been on the UCW food committee, but she says not and that I always get things mixed up. All I remember is she was whomping up all those fancy sandwiches made into wheels and checkerboards with their edges dipped in parsley, but it was worth our lives if any of us kids dared touch one. She never made anything like that for us. For us it was slabs of roast beef and pork, huge potatoes baked in their skins, vats of rice pudding. I can see now she was cooking for Dad and Henry who, from the time he was sixteen, worked as hard as Dad. And Dad was the sort of man who, if you put a normal-sized slice of bread in front of him, such as sliced store bread, would look at it in bewilderment that was sincere, wondering what he was expected to do with it.

What Mother was trying to tell me that August evening, the word she was having trouble saying, was *suicide*. She could not say it around Dad because he would tell her she was being a "silly old woman." Actually, Mother couldn't bring herself to say that word even when Dad wasn't around. What she finally did say, through frequent pauses, was that maybe Francie hadn't done what she might have to save herself. "Remember," said Mother, stretching up her eyebrows and looking into her coffee cup, "that time we just about went down to the basement?"

By now it was late. In order to speak of Francie uninterrupted we had to outwait Dad's bedtime, which is usually about nine. Finally, at eleven he stood up and said he couldn't take any more and hadn't we better go to bed, too, but Mother told him there was no way any man was going to tell her when to go to bed, so we didn't. Before leaving the room, he put his head close to mine and raised one hand. He said he wanted me to remember one word. "Vacuum cleaner," he said, then brought his hand down. He repeated softly, "Vacuum cleaner." He turned to Mother, "Don't forget to tell her about the vacuum cleaner."

I looked across the chrome table top at Mother. By now we were inside, the mosquitoes being too much for us also. "What does he mean by that?" I asked.

"Oh," she said. "There was something about a vacuum cleaner. Some evidence... And Bobby said something. But that's not the point. Your father never sees the point."

I could see why Dad was upset with Mother. There was no basis of fact to what she was hinting. I could also see Mother's point. Plain facts don't tell the truth.

Mother has trouble with fluid retention. Her hands and ankles were swollen in the heat. Still, she keeps her fingernails rounded and the same length. She always wears pink nail polish. She is careful with her hair, perfectly white now, even though at that moment it was wispy because of the heat and the effort of making us supper. She set her cup in its saucer. Her face was lowered, a face once young and lovely, now old and, to any impartial observer, unlovely. I felt a surge of feeling for her. After all, she dealt with fear the way most people do, by denying the existence of the feared object. As long as she could deny it, she would be all right. The people in trouble are the ones who can't distance themselves from the images they see in their dark moments.

Francie was like that, although of course I didn't know it for a long time. At that shower she didn't look any different than half the girls in Hackett. She wore spike heels and dangly earrings and had her hair done up in one of those beehives that were popular back then. I remember thinking she was "with it." That made me wonder about Stan, since I never considered him a "with it" guy. I mean Stan was all right. When he put on a tie and a sportscoat and went to town he looked great. He was blond and tanned from being outside. He had a great build from all that farm work. He had a neat car and his dancing was perfect. I didn't know about his dancing then, because there was no way he would ever dance with a twelve-year-old cousin. Later though, throughout the years, at weddings

and such, we danced. His steps and rhythm were so regular you could
all but fall asleep and not miss a step. He could go on like that, never
wavering, all night. You could see it got on Francie's nerves. He liked the
two-step, the polka and foxtrot. She would rather have been rocking.

When I started taking an interest in Francie I was sixteen, at that sappy
romantic age when all you do is philosophize about love, arriving at grand,
eloquent, and completely erroneous conclusions. To me, Francie was
glamour itself, maybe it was her perfume, her accent, or the high heels
she still wore. By then I had my driver's license, and I would go over to
see her on weekends, sometimes in the evening. It was only six miles.

Francie was a London girl. She never would have thought of coming
to Canada if it hadn't been for her two friends at the typing agency, Queenie
and Mary. Apparently, these three girls would go to the pictures together
and whatever else English girls do for excitement. During lunch breaks
they would talk some more, and finally they all convinced each other that
seeing a bit of the world would get them out of the typing agency. Their
destination was Calgary because Mary had a cousin here, but neither Mary
nor Queenie stayed very long. Queenie went on to Vancouver, and Mary
ended up in Australia. Maybe Francie married Stan because going to live
on a thousand acres at the edge of the Palliser triangle seemed like an
equally daring adventure, something like the Australian Outback. When
I was sixteen I didn't think that, of course. I realized people got married
because they fell madly in love and couldn't help themselves.

Francie and I had some good times that summer. She showed me how
to do my face and hair. She had more bottles and jars than a drugstore.
One intriguing concoction was called after-five pickup. You smeared it on
your face, relaxed twenty minutes while it dried, then splashed it off with
cold water. It was supposed to do wonders for your skin. I remember
once, after it dried, catching my reflection in the mirror. I just about dropped
from shock. My face had changed into a death mask with two dark holes
for eyes.

As for Francie, she was so full of life you felt more alive just being around
her. Instead of walking, she swished. She always had some plan or in-
trigue on the go. She was sewing herself a bikini to wear to the official
opening of the new Hackett Sports Complex and Swimming Pool because
she couldn't find anything brief enough at McLeod's. She had just ordered
a gourmet cookbook through the mail and intended serving Stan something
different from it every night. She put on her face every morning, winking

her false eyelashes and saying how you never know who might come to the door. She wore short skirts and crossed her legs a lot.

I now realize Francie was fighting for her life that summer. Her in-laws, my Aunt Mildred and Uncle Hugh, lived across the road, and whenever they were around, particularly Aunt Mildred, Francie was especially flippant and wild-eyed. By this time she had a couple of kids, and Aunt Mildred liked to say she got worse with each one. It seemed the more tethers to limit her, the more frenzied she became.

When I went back to school that fall I got my first boyfriend, steady that is. Well, fairly steady. It was probably thanks to Francie and all her creams and lotions. But then I didn't have time for much else but Jay and my homework and not much for my homework. Of course, I still had chores at home. Only death might have relieved me of those. So I didn't see a lot of Francie ever again. I mean we met in town, and I'd go over to their place once in a while, and they'd come and have Sunday dinner with us sometimes, but I mean really see her and talk to her the way we did that summer, sitting up half the night on the back porch, smoking. We would look at the stars the way you can in the country without lights to interfere, and we'd talk about life and destiny.

I really don't know what happened to Francie, I mean inside. On the outside, it was like she just caved in. She got to be terribly thin. She stopped wearing any make-up, even lipstick. She never did anything with her hair. She dragged herself around like a dog with its hindquarters broken. Once, when she was walking toward me, along the sidewalk, I didn't recognize her and wondered who the old lady was. She had three more kids, five in all, and after each one she looked worse than before. By now I was away at university and knew words like *prophylactics*. I remember one Christmas when, large with new-found knowledge, disdainful of the unenlightened, I discussed the matter with Mother.

"Why does she keep on having those kids?" I asked.

"Well, she won't be having any more," Mother answered.

My ears perked, eager for gossip. But there was something about the way Mother had spoken, the purse of her lips. Suddenly I didn't want to know what they might have done to Francie for her own good.

Obviously, what was happening was not the average woman letting herself go in a boring marriage situation. "No, it's true," Mother agreed. "She can't seem to pull herself together. I went over there one day and there she was sitting in the middle of a mess like you wouldn't believe. You could see the kids had dressed themselves. Poor little Bobby had his shoes on the wrong feet and they weren't tied and he kept tripping on the laces and his little legs were filthy. And they were hungry. And there was the baby yelling in his crib, his diaper dirty." She stopped. She couldn't go on. It was too awful.

She couldn't talk to Mildred, either, because that was like waving a red flag in front of a bull. Mildred would start on a tirade of complaints that did nothing to help the situation. And no one wanted to talk to Stan. The consensus was he had enough problems.

The thing is there's nothing basically wrong with Stan. In a lot of ways he reminds me of Dad, solid and decent. But in other ways they're probably the same, too. It's not that they're intolerant of what they don't understand. It's just beyond them that anyone could have anything but a straightforward realistic outlook on life. And I think in the end, Francie was spooked by Stan the same way she was by the prairie.

One of the last times I saw her we were sitting in Mother's new kitchen. I refused to go out to their farm for a visit because it depressed me so much. The kids did all right, considering. A couple of them have jobs in Calgary now. And the house became cleaner and better organized when they were old enough to be in charge of things. But there was such a hollow lonely feeling in that house, as though nothing and nobody was connecting.

Anyway, we were in Mother's kitchen and the wind came up, the way it does out there where there's nothing to stop it. Francie was staring out the window, the one that faces nothing. She was looking high and far across those pitiful fences. When she turned back to me she had an expression on her face I recognized. That must have been what Dad saw in my face on the day of the storm. Pure panic. Her eyes were large. You could see a lot of white. She didn't say anything. I remember what Dad had done with me, so I reached out my hand to touch her arm. She pulled back. She turned her face away. Soon after she left.

Thinking of that time, I was starting to see how it might have been. Francie in her kitchen. Let Dad have his rational explanations; let her be vacuuming. Or maybe she doesn't hear the wind right away because it's always windy. Maybe she doesn't notice the darkness because for her it is always dark. Or maybe she does hear it coming. She does notice the sky, and she waits for the shape to twist out of the darkness, the gray funnel spiralling between earth and sky. She waits in the cold, in the terror of that strange atmosphere. When it arrives, she sees that the funnel is a solid mass like a wall. She knows she can't go around it or over it. She knows that the only way out is to go through it. She tells herself that it is only for a moment. She opens the door for it. She puts up her hands, not to hold it back but to welcome it. She feels herself light as a dry husk as she is picked up, as she travels the twisted centre up to the light. Then she is released. She is free. I decide that at the last moment she is not frightened at all.